My Heart Beats for You

My Heart Beats for You

Tina Marie

www.urbanbooks.net

Urban Books, LLC
300 Farmingdale Road, N.Y.-Route 109
Farmingdale, NY 11735

My Heart Beats for You Copyright © 2022 Tina Marie

All rights reserved. No part of this book may be repro-
duced in any form or by any means without prior consent
of the Publisher, except brief quotes used in reviews.

ISBN 13: 978-1-64556-330-3
ISBN 10: 1-64556-330-8

First Trade Paperback Printing April 2022
Printed in the United States of America

10 9 8 7 6 5 4 3 2 1

*This is a work of fiction. Any references or similarities
to actual events, real people, living or dead, or to real
locales are intended to give the novel a sense of reality.
Any similarity in other names, characters, places, and
incidents is entirely coincidental.*

Distributed by Kensington Publishing Corp.
Submit Orders to:
Customer Service
400 Hahn Road
Westminster, MD 21157-4627
Phone: 1-800-733-3000
Fax: 1-800-659-2436

R0462099679

My Heart Beats for You

by

Tina Marie

Acknowledgments

I would first like to thank God for giving me this gift of writing and for providing me with every blessing I have received thus far and will receive in the future.

I want to thank my family, my fiancé, Jay, for putting up with all the late nights and my crazy moods while I am writing. To my kids: Jashanti, Jaymarni, and Jasheer, I want you to know that I work so hard so you can have it all.

To my Cole Hart Presents team, salute to all of you for keeping on the grind and staying positive. Cole, the fact that you wanted me on your team means more to me than you will ever know. Princess, Anna, and Twyla: I swear you ladies are just amazing, and I love you! I want to thank all of my Pen Sisters no matter what company you are in for all of the love, support, and for always helping to push me to my next goal. I appreciate you all!

Ladora, you are the world's best little sister. I love you, and I believe in you always! Keep pushing. That number one is coming your way.

Natasha, we have been friends for what seems like forever, and now you're more like family. You could never be replaced in my life. You have seen me at my best and worst and still have my back. Oh, and you have learned to put up with all my moods. LOL. I love you, boo!

Natavia, only in a perfect world would I have thought that my favorite author would be my real-life friend. And even though this isn't a perfect world, I am so happy you became my friend. I value all the talks, laughs, wcc, and advice. Love you, soul sister (inside joke).

Coco, I didn't think I could write a dedication to you without crying. I was right. You are a bomb-a** little sister. I would go to war for you with anyone. The way you love on my son and have never turned your back on me is everything. You're filled with positivity and joy, and I can't find the words to thank you. I love you!

Sunni, there are so many days you have talked me off the ledge and just been a friend. I love your whole life. I could never replace you. Your bestseller is right around the corner. I can feel it!

Nisey, Quanisha, and Keke, you three have been rocking with me since forever and are the best admins ever. I love how you love me but most of all how you all have come to love each other. Tina, you may be new to the team, but you are a welcome addition! You ladies don't let me forget a thing and handle all the grunt work so I can write. XoXo! To my test readers, Kristi, Sweets, and Jammie, there would be no book without you ladies. You all are my blessings! Tootie and Liz, I couldn't ask for better promoters. One thing I learned in this business is it takes a team, and finding the two of you completed my team.

To my Baby Mama Zatasha, even though we are both crazy Geminis, I still love you, boo. Couldn't do this book ish without you!! And to all the Bookies, I appreciate the love and support you show all authors, not just me. It makes a difference having a place where we are respected, celebrated, and offered endless support!

To my friends and family: I appreciate all of the love and support. My cousins, Claire, Dionne, Donna, and Tanisha. My friends: Letitia, Natasha, Jennifer, Sharome, Shante, Diana, and Kia. I'm truly grateful for you all, and I love you. To my best friend, there will never be enough

Acknowledgments

letters in the alphabet to thank you for everything, so I won't even try.

To all of my fans, readers, test readers, admins, and anyone who has ever read or purchased my work, or shared a link or a book cover, you're all appreciated, and I promise to keep pushing on your behalf to write what you're looking for.

Chapter 1

Inaya

I could feel the heat from the sun wake me up. The sun represented hope for me, hope and a safe place. I was afraid of the dark, and most nights I stayed awake all night waiting for the sun to peek through the blinds before I could finally close my eyes and get some rest. I yawned as I cuddled closer to Kadia on the hard floor. I could feel her little legs stretching out until she was kicking me. She had her tiny arms wrapped around my neck, and I could feel the sweat from her body dripping onto me, mingling with my sweat. It was already hot before the sunbeams helped roast us further.

"Mmmm," Kadia whimpered in her sleep as she rolled onto her belly, and her head flopped off of the pillow and hit the carpeted floor. Only a kid would still sleep after their head bounced onto the rough carpet in a house that was a hundred-plus degrees inside. Slowly easing away from her so she wouldn't wake up, I sat against the side of the bed. These were the times the guilt threatened to drown me, but what could I do?

The alarm on my phone wouldn't stop going off, and I knew it was time to get Kadia ready for school while I was supposed to go on a job interview. I wanted to call my cousin Sahnai, but my battery was at 50 percent, and with the electricity off, I couldn't afford to let it die.

Just thinking of our new daily routine made the tears drip from my eyes. I hated hearing Kadia cry out when I had to wash her in the dark bathroom in cold water. She deserved better than that.

The electricity ran the water heater and the furnace and everything else we needed to survive in this place. We had beds in our own rooms, but I was afraid to let Kadia sleep in a pitch-black house in a room all alone. What if she got scared and tried to find me? She could fall down the stairs or trip over a toy on the floor and get hurt. As for the bed in my room, we slept on the floor because it was just too hot right now to sleep on a bed. Shit, heat rises.

Thank God the school provided breakfast and lunch for Kadia. I worked in a day care, so I also had those two meals provided for me. When it came to dinner, we struggled. Sometimes I went to the corner store and would buy us Hot Pockets and cold subs with my food stamp card, and then used the Arab store's microwave to heat up anything that needed to be warmed before we went home. The funny thing was I had over $1,000 in food stamps on my card, but I couldn't buy groceries because the fridge wouldn't work without electricity. So month after month, they just kept giving me food stamps, knowing I had nowhere to store the food. I used some of them to buy food for Kadia at my mother's house when she went over there. And I used the rest to buy us food from the corner store, but if I didn't use them by the next month, I would lose the old ones. They only stayed on the card for four months before they were forfeited back to the State.

On the nights I had class, I used the credit on my student ID to buy chips and snacks out of the vending machine. I swore those snacks would keep me awake, especially in my child psych class. I wasn't sure why that was needed to become a science teacher, but it was. The best thing about those nights while I was in class was that Kadia got to eat good at my mom's house, a real home-cooked dinner, and I was grateful for that.

"Kadia, Kadia. Wake up, baby," I told my 4-year-old daughter while gently picking her up off the floor. I took the time to run my hand over her pigtails, pushing the barrettes out of her face. My lips made smacking noises as I kissed her chubby little cheeks.

"Morning, Mama. I'm hungry and it's so hot. When will the fans work again?" She didn't even whine while asking. In my mind I was asking the same shit, but with a different attitude.

"Soon, baby. Mama is working on a new job," I said, while giving her a reassuring smile. I wished I could snap my fingers and just have the money to pay the light bill or buy anything Kadia wanted and needed. Unfortunately, life wasn't that easy. I was lucky if I got thirty hours a week at the day care, and I only made $8 an hour, which was barely enough to put gas in the car to get to work and school and pay my portion of the rent. I knew someday this would not still be our situation, but today it was.

As I looked in the mirror using my phone as a flash-light, I still saw a pretty face staring back, except this pretty face was tired. My light brown eyes looked droopy, and my eyebrows were bushy. My light skin didn't have a glow to it anymore. Instead it looked pale and chalky. Even my cheeks had a sunken look to them. A few days ago, I'd overheard two of my classmates talking about me after my teaching seminar course. The ugly redhead asked the ashy one if she thought I was on drugs. They'd decided at the end of the conversation that must be why I looked unkempt and had lost so much weight. They sealed the deal with a sad shake of their heads and a laugh. Honestly I didn't know whether to be angry or just sad. But I didn't even have the energy to entertain their nonsense. I wasn't a punk, but there was no explanation for my circumstances to the outside world, so I let it go.

Mechanically, I took the brush and the brown gel and pulled my long black hair into a ponytail. Next, I added a clip so it wasn't smothering me in this heat. I wanted to use the concealer I had to cover the bags under my eyes, but let's be honest, I was using a cell phone light to see, so fuck it, and I would probably end up looking worse. Running my hands down my thin frame, smoothing the blouse and pencil skirt I had on as best I could, I tried to smile one more time. Looking at the time, I realized we were going to be late if I didn't hurry up. Almost tripping as I rushed and slid my feet into my nude Aldo heels, I grabbed the manila folder holding copies of my résumé and ran down the stairs.

"Kadia, let's go. Your bus is coming," I yelled unnecessarily since she was already skipping down the stairs with her princess bookbag on and in her neatly pressed private-school uniform. My baby was a good girl. I rarely had to yell at her, and she was pretty quiet.

Quickly stepping outside my front door, I ran into a hard body. "Shit, I'm so sorry," I said, looking up into a face wearing a deep frown. He was fine, don't get me wrong, but he looked mean as fuck. He had chinky eyes and chocolate brown skin, and his hair was pulled into a ponytail on the top of his head. He had on a black hoodie half covering his face, True Religion jeans that looked brand new, and a pair of black Timberlands. *Who the hell wears a black hoodie in this heat?* He must have been at least six feet tall because he was towering over my five-foot, six-inch frame. He gave me a glare and a nod as he began walking past me into the townhouse right next door.

"Mommy said, 'Sorry,' and you did not say, 'That's okay,'" Kadia chimed in before his hand could put the key in the door.

"Kadia, it's all right. It was Mommy's fault. Let's go, baby," I harshly whispered to her as I began dragging her down the path. Before I could get far, he was in front of me again with a deeper scowl on his face. This morning was really not going well for me at all. As he looked down at Kadia's little face, I just knew he was going to scare her with all of his frowning and mean looks. He was probably about to say something rude to her, and then I was going to have to stand up for my baby.

Instead he smiled, and one dimple popped out on his right cheek. I noticed his teeth were white and in a straight row.

"Hey, little one, you're right. I'm sorry I did not accept your mommy's apology. I wasn't thinking. Can you forgive me?"

Kadia really cocked her head to the side and put one finger to her cheek as she looked up to the sky in thought. I wished she would hurry up, because I just knew this nigga was about to get annoyed. I knew firsthand that some men did not have patience for kids.

"Okay, we forgive you," she finally said after what seemed like forever, and then she held out her hand for him to shake it. Surprisingly he did so while still smiling at her.

"Have a good day at school, little mama. I hope you learn a lot," he said, and then he was gone, almost like he was never there.

"Mama, we are going to miss the bus," Kadia said, snapping me out of my fantasy.

Great! My new neighbor looked like the thug of my dreams but probably thought I was an idiot for running into him and then allowing my child to hold a conversation with him when he was clearly annoyed.

As soon as Kadia stepped on her bus, I was speed walking to my gold Maxima, hoping it would start today with no issues. Saying a little prayer, I turned the key and heard the engine turn over. *Phew.* I didn't want to be late, because I really needed this job so I could get my and my baby's lives together. We couldn't keep living like this. She wasn't used to this kind of life, and she had never been without lights or hot water before now. We had never been rich, but I never allowed her to know we were poor.

I made sure she had a comfortable home and clean clothes that fit, as well as hot meals every day. I didn't know where things went so wrong. Well, I did. When I decided to get better for me and Kadia was when things seemed to get more complicated. By "better," I mean not allowing us to be in an unhealthy situation anymore. Money couldn't buy comfort, good health, or a person's safety. Money or lack of money could make doing what was right even harder to do.

As soon as I pulled into the parking lot of Saber Solutions, I could feel my palms get sweaty. I had no idea why I was interviewing for this internship. Though it was entry level, I had no idea what they did at this company. Based on the aqua-tinted glass windows surrounding the modern-looking building, it was something I didn't have experience in. I felt way out of my league. Glancing at myself in the mirror one more time before getting out of the car, I whispered a little prayer and went to take a chance on my future.

Walking into the lobby, I stopped at the front desk, where the very blond secretary asked with a confused look on her face if she could help me.

"I have a nine a.m. interview with a Mr. Tyler," I responded, making sure to smile and give her eye contact. Even though she was looking at me like I was a spider or dirt on her shoe, I kept my head up with confidence. This was my big chance, and I was taking it.

"Someone will be with you shortly," she responded with an attitude. I stood waiting since she didn't offer me a seat. Luckily Mr. Tyler walked out and introduced himself before my feet began to hurt in those high-ass heels. You know what they say: beauty is pain. I could see him giving Miss Blondie an angry look, so maybe he was not pleased that she left me standing at the front like a delivery girl.

Mr. Tyler was the vice president of operations at Saber Solutions. I wasn't yet sure what operations he was running, but I couldn't wait to find out. He had on a gray suit with a crisp white shirt and an aqua-green tie that matched his light-colored eyes. The interview was surprisingly painless. Mr. Tyler was very down-to-earth for a VP, or at least I thought so because he asked if I had kids. He talked a little about his twin sons and how the company was family oriented, and hearing that made me want the job even more. He explained that I scored in the top percentile on the test his company had anyone interested in a position take with the application. To me, this didn't seem like a big deal, and I told him so, but he explained that only 5 percent of applicants even made it past the mid-range of this test. He told me I would be informed of his decision by the end of the week, as they still had to check my references. He then sent me on my way with a hopeful smile on my face and a prayer in my heart. This job would solve so many issues for me and my daughter. I would not have to worry about money or not enough hours again.

On my way back to the lobby from Mr. Tyler's office, I noticed the employees at their desks and in their offices. Everyone looked happy while they typed away at their computers or talked on their desk phones. This place felt right for me. No more working with troubled kids or ratchet coworkers. As I reached the door to the lobby, deep inside, I wanted to turn around and cry out that I needed a decision right away. I wanted to tell him I could no longer allow my child to live like she was, with no hot water or TV, not even a night-light, but instead I thanked Mr. Tyler and walked out to my car, again praying it would start so I could make it to my job. I told them I had a dentist appointment and that was why I would be late today. If I had told them I was looking for a new job, I was sure they would have let me go, and that wasn't something I could handle right now.

Chapter 2

Phantom

Fuck, I didn't mean to make the little girl feel bad this morning. Honestly I didn't even notice her with her little ponytails swinging and her big brown eyes. I was too focused on her mother. Even with her looking like she'd missed a few meals and like she was carrying the weight of the world on her shoulders, I knew she was pretty. I could tell the long hair she had pulled up with all those clips and other girly shit was her own, and even with her skinny arms and legs, her breasts and ass were sitting up nice. Her face was cute with honey brown eyes and a beauty mark on her top lip. It was light, but I could see it through her pink lip gloss.

It had been a long time since a girl really caught my eye. Maybe it was because she had on professional clothes. That had to be it. I was used to these bitches walking around in tiny shorts and even tinier shirts showing everything that God gave them, usually throwing it directly my way, I guess hoping I would fall and bump my fucking head and wife one of their ho asses.

Honestly, this wasn't the first time I'd noticed li'l shawty from next door. I'd lived there a few weeks, and I kept odd hours due to my "profession," so I saw her when she was leaving most mornings. I would just be getting in sometimes, and she was usually running down the path in her tight-ass jeans and a yellow T-shirt, which had a colorful stick-figure kid on it. Seemed like a uniform for a day care or a camp or some shit. I noticed her coming home late on Tuesdays and Thursdays struggling to carry her sleeping daughter and a bookbag that looked like it weighed more than her.

Even though I wasn't interested in settling down with any female, especially not one with a kid, there was something about her, and li'l mama was a charmer. She made me think about the baby I never got to know. If I hadn't heard her speak today, I would not have known she could talk at all. She was always pretty silent.

The first week I moved here, I didn't even know anyone lived in the townhouse next door. I never heard any noise. Not a vacuum or a TV. And there was a whole kid living there. I would have expected to hear running and playing and shit breaking, shawty yelling, or something. My sister had three boys, and those fuckers hadn't been quiet a day in their lives. The oldest one was deaf, and his ass still found a way to make noise.

On the real, I'd just come from killing somebody before I'd gotten there, but I didn't think it was obvious to anyone. I hoped I didn't have blood on my face or some shit, because shawty was dragging li'l mama down the path like she was scared of a nigga. Right before they rounded the corner, I saw a tiny hand reach up and wave. I waved back and then headed into the crib with a smile on my face.

As soon as I got inside, I took a shower and began thinking about the morning's events. I realized I liked li'l mama. She was a little feisty, but she seemed like a sweet kid. I was going to make it a point to buy her some ice cream or some shit when those trucks be coming around to our complex to make up for what she thought was my rude behavior. I guess people didn't expect me to, but I loved kids. Shit, I even had one once, until my ex, Shawnie . . . well, anyway, I had a daughter, but she wasn't here anymore, and Shawnie was one of the reasons a nigga like me would never settle down or trust a bitch.

Today took a lot of energy out of me. Not really because of the activity of killing someone, but because of the amount of anger I had inside for the person who crossed me. Keeping these niggas in line was hard work, and I wasn't the type to let another motherfucker handle my business, because that was when problems occurred. I just couldn't trust the job to be done right, and when dealing with murder, I wasn't taking any chances, because that shit will come back to you if not done correctly.

Fuck. As soon as I got out of the shower and dried off, I decided to lie down for a while. Once my head hit the pillow, I couldn't even sleep. All I kept thinking about was shorty from next door. I didn't even know this chick's name, and she was already invading my mind. I wondered what she was doing today since it didn't look like she was following her regular routine. Maybe she had traffic court or some shit since she was dressed up. *I have to find out her name. Fuck.* I felt this urge to text her and see if she was good, but a nigga didn't even have her number. I had to get on that.

"Yo, nigga, you gonna sleep all day or what?" Lox yelled as he stomped up the stairs.

Rolling my eyes, I didn't even bother to respond and tell this nigga I never made it to sleep. I just made my way to my bathroom and brushed my teeth and splashed some water on my face. I swore Lox's ass slept like two hours a day. It'd been that way since we were kids. I wondered if he were part robot or some shit. Like, who the fuck can live on barely any sleep? Not the kid! I be taking naps and all to catch up on mine.

After I showered, I threw on some plaid Polo shorts and a white V-neck tee, then slid my feet into some brown leather Polo sandals. Once I threw on my Rolex and earrings and sprayed on my Gucci Made to Measure cologne, I was ready to go.

Lox and I kicked it for a while before I was ready to put my little plan in motion.

"Lox I'ma touch the road for a bit. I will check you later, my nigga," I yelled to my cousin as I made my way outside.

I really didn't have anywhere to go, but I was trying to time going outside with when shorty next door got her daughter off the bus. I just wanted to hear her voice for a few before I hit the streets. As soon as I rounded the corner toward the parking lot, I saw the bus pull up and li'l mama running around her mom, giggling and showing her a paper that she must have been proud of. As soon as she spotted me, she began running my way. It was almost funny watching the look on her mom's face. It was one of horror as she tried to call out to her.

"Kadia, no. Come back here now!" she yelled even though Kadia wasn't listening to shit she had to say.

"Hello, mister. Look what I made in school," she said, at the same time showing me a picture of the letter K that I assumed she wrote and then colored. "K is for Kadia," she sang, running around and waving her paper.

"I did not get a chance to introduce myself to you earlier. I was tired from work. I am Phantom, and I heard that your name is Kadia. I think your picture is nice. Did you make it all by yourself?" I asked, crouching down to take a closer look.

Feeling her shadow and smelling her Victoria's Secret body spray, I knew her mother was right there. I took a moment before I got up. I didn't want to like her or any girl. I just wanted to fuck 'em and leave 'em. But something about her made my senses come alive whenever she was around.

"Phantom, we are sorry to disturb you. I am Inaya, and this is my daughter, Kadia, who is four and does not know any better than to keep bothering you. We will be on our way now, right, Kadia?" she said while she was giving little mama that look only a mother can give. The one that says, "Let's go now."

"Inaya," I slowly said her name like I could taste it across my tongue. Damn, she was giving me a look like I was crazy. I mean, I was, but not the way she was probably thinking. "Iny, if it's okay, I came out here to catch you two. I wanted to treat Kadia to ice cream as an 'I'm sorry' for this morning. We can run across the street and go to the place next to the park if you have the time."

"Please, Mommy, can we?" Kadia begged her mother while jumping from one foot to the other, her ponytails swinging so hard I thought she was going to hit herself in the face.

I could see it in her eyes she wanted to say no, but I guess making Kadia happy won out, because she slightly nodded her head and turned toward the ice cream shop. Shit, I was supposed to be buying li'l mama ice cream from the truck, but I didn't want to leave their presence. Inaya was interesting, and I wanted to know more about her, and Kadia made me smile.

"Hey, Phantom, who the fuck is Iny?" she asked with a serious face as we walked across the road.

"That's what I'ma call you. Iny. It's my nickname for you. Whatcha thought, I didn't pay your name any attention?" I asked, raising my eyebrow.

"Hmm," she said, turning to walk up to the window as she faced the cashier at the ice cream spot. "She will have a small vanilla cone with rainbow sprinkles," she told the cashier with a slight smile on her face.

"Ma, get what you want, too."

"Nah, I'm good," she replied.

"Mommy likes cookie dough ice cream with sprinkles," Kadia said with a grin. Kids were good for telling all ya business.

"You heard the little one," I instructed the lady taking our order.

"Phantom, what about you? Don't you like ice cream?" Kadia asked with wide, innocent eyes. I could tell she was used to getting her way because she was cute.

Shit, I ain't had ice cream since I was a kid, but the look on Kadia's face, one of anticipation, led me to order strawberry ice cream with all kinds of candies that she suggested I get. I thought she wanted to have them because she asked to taste each one.

This ice cream tasted like the best I had ever had, maybe because of the people keeping me company while I ate it. *Fuck, I got to stay away from this bitch. She got me feeling soft as a motherfucker.*

As soon as we finished and had walked back across the road, both of my phones began ringing like crazy. I only answered Lox.

"Yo, what's up, son? I'ma meet you at the car in a few. I'm right across the road."

"Thank you, Phantom. You really didn't have to do that," Inaya said as they turned to walk toward their crib.

"Thank you, Mr. Phantom," Kadia said politely, then gave me a hug and ran off in the direction of home.

"Inaya," I said one more time softly in the air before I hopped in my silver Audi and sped off.

Chapter 3

Inaya

I woke up with him on my mind today. I didn't know what to think of him now. *Mr. Phantom, hmm. So much for my mean-ass neighbor.* He seemed to be sweet on kids, I guessed. He was somewhat nice to me, but I thought it was just because of Kadia. She had a way of charming everyone who met her. I thought one of the reasons was because she was very intelligent for her age and knew what to say and when.

Since we officially met him a few weeks ago, he'd made it a point to speak to Kadia almost every day. He bought her ice cream and doughnuts, and he even picked her up a Barbie doll, talking about he saw it when he was at Walmart and just grabbed it. Okay, what was this nigga doing in the toy aisle? Shit, I couldn't even picture him in no damn Walmart. I was sure he had hoes to do his shopping for him.

For some reason he didn't have much to say to me though. I thought he was trying to get to me through my daughter. Even if he didn't want to date me or make a commitment, I thought he would have at least tried to fuck already. When he saw me, it was usually, "How is Kadia doing?" or, "Where is li'l mama?" On the nights I had school, he made sure to come outside and carry Kadia or my books to the door. If she wasn't sleeping already, I walked along, listening to them talk about their day, and I would daydream about him turning to me and touching my hand or kissing my lips, but that never happened.

As I was sorting the laundry to take to the wash, I could still smell his Gucci cologne on Kadia's shirt. *It must be from when she hugged him yesterday.* I couldn't help but hold her tiny white button-down shirt up to my nose and breathe in deeply. There was something about Phantom when he looked at me that made my whole soul weak.

As soon as I got the last of the clothes sorted, I carried my baskets to the car so I could get this chore done before Kadia got home from school. I hated taking her to the laundry place. It was dirty and she got restless. When little kids get restless, they start to touch everything.

Once I got there and started to wash, I scrolled CareerBuilder for jobs, clicking quick apply to everything that paid more than the day care.

Eventually I broke down and called my cousin while folding the clothes. I always brought my iron to the laundromat so I could press all of Kadia's school uniforms since I couldn't plug it in at home. Sometimes people stared at me funny, but I didn't give a fuck. Making sure my baby was straight was my priority, not what the next person thought. Popping the trunk on the Maxima, I loaded all the clothes in the car so I could head home.

As soon as I pulled into the parking lot, I realized my phone was only at 30 percent. *Damn it.* I needed it to be at least 80 to get me through the day in case a job called and to use for the alarm the next morning. I kept the car running and plugged my phone back into the car charger. This situation was wearing on me more each day. I couldn't ask my mother for any help. She wasn't that kind of mother, and we didn't have that kind of relationship. She would throw any help she would give me in my face and tell me how worthless I was. That was why I didn't discuss anything with her that went on in my life. I didn't ask her to babysit either. Kadia went over there with my grandmother, who just happened to live with my mother, on my school nights.

I must have dozed off waiting for the phone to charge, because before I knew it, Phantom was banging on the window of my car. *What the fuck? He's acting like he is the police or something.*

"Yo, shawty. What you doing just sittin' in the car like that? You okay?"

"Yeah. I was just chillin' before I carry this laundry in. It's hot you know."

I didn't want to tell him I had to charge my phone in the car because I had no electricity in my house. I could tell by the way he was looking around the car that he wasn't convinced by what I said.

"Where is Kadia?" he asked finally, like I was hiding her somewhere in here with me. Maybe the glove box or something the way his eyes kept searching my shit.

"At school, Phantom. Where else would she be this time of the day? Nigga, you act like I stuffed her in the trunk or she is under the seat. You got your eyes shifting all over my car like you looking for something."

"Tell li'l mama I said what's up," he threw at me as he walked away with a smirk on his face.

Well, I guess it's a good thing he is no fucking gentleman and didn't bother to ask me if he could help carry my laundry. He was a nosy motherfucker though. *Who cares if I sit in my car? That's my business.* That fucker. I could have been having some outside freaky phone sex for all he knew.

I dragged the laundry to the front door and had just enough time to put it in the doorway and run to the bus stop to pick up Kadia. As soon as I got her off the bus, she seemed down. I hoped she wasn't getting depressed because of our situation. She had been handling it all really well so far, playing games with the flashlight, enjoying sleeping with me every night, and eating out all the time. Today though, she came off the bus dragging her bag behind her and walking with her head down. This wasn't the Kadia I knew.

"Sweetie, are you okay? Did someone at school make you sad?" I was in full mommy mode ready to bust someone's head at that school.

"No, Mommy, I'm okay. School was fun. We learned about fire and what to do if there is a fire. I had my ballet class today, and I'm going to be one of the lead dancers in our next performance."

I stopped her before we got to the door and took her face in my hands.

"Kadia, I know it is hard not having lights or a TV in the house, and Mommy promises that it will not be like this forever. I don't want you to be sad. In a few weeks the lights will be on, and Mommy will take you shopping and get you a new doll." I expected her to smile or something. Instead she just nodded and kept walking, and I was praying in my head that my school check would be on time this semester so I could get us out of this situation we were in.

"There is Princess Kadia. How are you today, li'l mama?" Phantom asked while standing in his doorway. Kadia ran over to him and gave him a hug and a slight smile. She then slowly walked back to me and grabbed my hand. "Yo, why she looking all sad and shit? I hope you ain't beat her. Did Mommy beat you, Kades?"

"Phantom, seriously? Why would I beat her? She just got off the school bus. I think she is just tired. It is hard for her to sleep well in this heat."

"Inaya, we have central air in these townhouses. Don't be beating on my li'l mama or I'ma fuck you up. That's my li'l homie right there, and I know she is a good girl. Kades, it wasn't no one at school messin' wit' you, was it?"

"No, Phantom, I am okay," she responded in a low voice.

"Iny, you know her teachers, right? Maybe we should call the school and see if these teachers are on the up and up. I ain't playin' that touchy-feely shit wit' baby girl, ya heard me?" This nigga was in my face and serious as hell.

"Whatever," I replied while rolling my eyes. I didn't even get into why we didn't use the central air, and I had no idea why he thought "we" needed to call anyone. "Phantom, I will call the school in the morning to make sure she didn't have any incidents today with any of the other students." I gave in because he did have me thinking about how well I really knew what happened at Kadia's school. I would rather be safe than sorry. I wasn't with her all day, and I be seeing hella shady shit on the news.

I had picked up sandwiches from Subway and juice and cookies for dinner when I was out earlier, but Kadia went to bed without eating and way before bedtime. As soon as my mind began to think it, the worst happened.

"Mommy, I can't breathe." She came into the kitchen holding her little chest, struggling to get air in her tiny lungs.

After trying the inhaler for a few minutes, I could see this was too far gone. She was gasping, and her chest was heaving up and down. This damn humidity was not helping her asthma, and I had no electricity to use her nebulizer. I decided to go knock on my neighbor's door. She was an older lady and was usually home unless she went to bingo.

Knock, knock, knock. "Miss Gina, please open the door. It's an emergency," I cried out.

"Yo, why you banging on the door like that?" nosy-ass Phantom asked while he and some guy with dreads walked up to his door. *Damn, wasn't his ass just leaving a little while ago?* As much as I was annoyed at seeing him, I was also grateful.

"Phantom, please help. It's Kadia. She can't breathe, and I need to hook up her machine. Miss Gina isn't answering, and I don't have any electricity at my place," I spit out while crying and holding Kadia in my arms. Before I knew it, I could feel him grabbing Kadia out of my arms and shoving past the guy with the dreads into his place. I slowly followed, still in shock that this was happening right now.

"Iny, where is the fucking machine?" he yelled at me, breaking me out of my trance. I handed it over with shaky hands, and he soon had the mask on her face, and she was coming around a little. I still called an ambulance because she was wheezing, but she was no longer heaving and turning blue. Seeing her like that scared me to the point where I could barely breathe.

I should have known she wasn't feeling well today when she came home from school and was so quiet. As soon as the ambulance got there, Phantom took over, shoving me in the back to ride with Kadia and demanding to know what hospital she was being taken to, all while yelling at the scared driver. He slammed the door behind us and shouted that he would see us there.

As soon as we pulled up, he was hopping out of a two-door black-on-black Bentley. That thing was so fast it looked like he beat the ambulance with sirens blaring and all. He hopped back in when he saw me and swung into one of the emergency parking spots, then jumped back out. The next moment he was next to us, holding Kadia's hand telling her she would be all right.

Once they took her in the back, I had to stop at the desk to fill out all the paperwork. As I flipped to the last page, I could feel his eyes on me, and I hesitantly looked up. I was immediately sorry I did, because if looks could kill, I would be dead. His chinky eyes were narrowed into a glare, and his nose was crinkled. He had his arms folded as if he was trying not to hit me. This was worse than his normal frowns and rude stares.

"So for real you got my li'l mama living in a crib wit' no fucking electricity? No lights, no food, not even a fucking fan in this heat?"

I picked up my head and started to explain. "I—"

"Nah, I ain't done yet. You are just another dumb-ass female living off the State and probably got an innocent baby daddy sending you coins, and you can't even do what's right for your kid. Inaya, I thought you were different. I was starting to actually like you, but now I see you worse than the average bitch. I mean, at least they can keep the lights on," he shouted at me while everyone in the waiting room looked at me like I was the worst mother in the world.

I hung my head and cried. I didn't even try to defend myself anymore. I really liked Phantom. He was the first man I allowed in my space and around my daughter since her dad. He had started to say hello to me this week and even smiled a little yesterday when I was walking to my car leaving for work. We didn't date or hang out much, but I was enjoying whatever we had, and now that was gone. He hated me. *Worse, he thinks I am a bad mother.*

"Family of Kadia Walker," the doctor called out as he walked into the waiting room.

Before I had time to react, Phantom was dragging me in his direction and demanding to see Kadia.

"Sir, who are you to the patient?"

I could see him getting more agitated as the doctor just stood there waiting for us to respond. I would think it was pretty obvious that one of us was her parent since a parent had to fill out the paperwork.

As soon as I went to speak, here came Phantom's crazy ass. "I am Jahdair, and I need you to take me to my daughter, Kadia, now!"

The doctor shrugged his shoulders. He probably noticed the pissed-off vibe Phantom was wearing like a coat, or maybe it was the bulge under his shirt from his gun. He walked us back while explaining she was given oxygen and doing well and that her breathing was normal, but they would need to keep her a few days for observation. And she would be getting a different prescription for her inhaler, one that was stronger.

Kadia smiled as soon as she saw both of us, and she held her arms up to Phantom . . . or, I should say, Jahdair. His real name was stuck in my head like a song playing over and over.

"Mommy, don't cry. You're the best mommy ever, and I love you," she said as I held her tiny hand. This made me break down and cry even more. I guessed I was a bad mom. My daughter almost died because of me. I had to figure this light shit out ASAP.

"Kadia, I will be back to see you in the morning, okay, mama? You get better and take care of Mommy, and I will bring you a surprise."

"Anything I want, Phantom?"

"Anything you want, Kades."

"I want roller skates," she replied with a big, goofy smile.

"Okay, roller skates it is," he replied as he gave Kadia a hug. He leaned down and whispered in my ear, "Stop fucking crying, yo. You gonna make her sad."

With that he walked right out the door. I wished I were getting a hug too. I could have used one or some comfort. I needed someone to let me know everything would be all right. Instead, I curled up in the chair next to Kadia and turned on the hospital TV before I fell asleep.

Chapter 4

Phantom

As soon as I left the hospital, I drove to the nearest Toys "R" Us before they locked the doors. After searching through what felt like a million aisles of toys, I decided to ask someone for some help.

"Sir, do you need a cart?" this big-booty caramel-colored chick asked.

"Yeah, I guess, and I need roller skates. Some pretty joints, pink and sparkly and shit."

As soon as she came back with the cart and I followed her to the right spot, she made a huge deal of bending over in front of me to pick the skates up. Shawty was all right. I guessed I could smash and dash her ass. She could have done better on her hair, but I ain't fucking her hair, so all was well.

"Sir, this is a lot of toys for one child. Are you sure you would like to purchase all of them?" she questioned me after dropping the skates in the cart with some other shit I picked up for Kades. I followed her to check out and almost laughed in her face. This ho was really trying to see how long my money was.

"Yo, ma, listen. I ain't ask you to tell me shit about what I am buying my li'l one, feel me? She is the only female digging in these pockets, so don't even get no dumb ideas.

Just ring this shit up and slide me your digits so I can slide up in them drawers when I feel like it."

Nothing else was said from her smart ass until she gave me my receipt with her number scribbled on it. *Just like I thought.* All she wanted was to get at the kid. She was probably trying to see if I had a wife at home or some shit.

Smirking, I made my way to my whip with the cart overflowing. I could barely see over the top of that shit. I knew I probably seemed like a soft-ass nigga, but there was just something about Kadia. She had my heart. I wished she were my little girl, and thinking about the bullshit I found out today really pissed me off. *How her slack-ass mama got her in there living like that and shit?* These bitches killed me.

As soon as I came home and started dragging all this shit inside with me, Lox was looking at a nigga with his eyebrows raised, and I just knew he was about to talk shit.

"What you looking at, ol' homely-ass-looking nigga? Baby girl is in the hospital, so I got her a few things to make her smile," I responded to his nosy-ass stare.

"Damn, man, you fucking her mama or some shit, son? Yo, she must got that good good. You whipped." My cousin was laughing so hard his ass tipped too far back in the chair, and he hit his head on the handle of the patio door.

"Nigga, that's what you get, and hell naw, I ain't smashin' her mama. If I could even tell you about this slack-ass bitch. She know her li'l one has asthma, and she got her over there wit' no fucking electricity. How you can't make it a priority to pay the damn light bill? I bet that bitch house dirty as hell, too. She probably a ho and can't find no nigga to help her out anymore. The pussy probably dried up like an old prune, and she couldn't beg a nigga like me to slide up in that."

"Son, did she say why or what happened? Maybe she had something wrong with her or just hit a rough patch," Lox said, trying to straighten shit out for shawty, but fuck that. I ain't hearing any of it. I was well acquainted with her type.

"Naw, man, fuck that. There are no excuses. She is just like the rest of these hoes. She just like my mama and baby mama. They all the fucking same, and that's why I ain't gonna never settle wit' none of 'em. Sad part is that this one is not even worth me fucking or letting her suck me off. Bad mothers are the worst in my book. She can go die in the street for all I care," I responded, cutting my eyes and leaving the room, not giving Lox a chance to respond.

Later, I dragged all the toys and a big-ass teddy bear to my truck so I could go check on my li'l homie. Before I got to the hospital, I decided to stop at Burger King and grab baby girl a meal and a milkshake. Shit, all kids loved those little meals with the toys. My nephews tore those shits up. They be pissed like a mother though because they'd have to wait to eat until they get home. I didn't play about my whips. Not even my granny could eat in my shit.

As soon as I walked in, I let my eyes scan the room and was relieved I didn't see Iny there. I didn't want to see her and start feeling sorry for her. She had those big brown puppy eyes that looked just like Kades's, and I wasn't interested in falling victim to her lies. Even as mad as I was, there was still a part of me that wanted to know where she was and what she was doing.

Once I opened the door wider and let the cart filled with toys be seen, baby girl's eyes lit up like an adult who won the lotto.

"Phantom, you didn't have to give me soooo many toys. I think I should only take the skates I asked for, and maybe the teddy bear so I won't be lonely while I am here," she said, looking sad all of the sudden.

"Naw, Kades, all of this is for you. You deserve them for being such a brave girl."

After she ate her food and played, I read her a few stories and watched her drift off to sleep.

"Mommy's gonna be mad," she whispered as she closed her eyes.

"I don't care," I whispered back as I kissed her on her head and tickled her until she giggled a little.

"Sir, can we get you guys anything? Maybe she needs a drink or some lunch?" this ratchet, loud-ass nurse asked as she strolled in the room, giving me what she thought was a sexy look. She was smacking her lips, which were smothered in blue lipstick, looking like she was eating a fucking Smurf. I could feel myself shudder and hold in a laugh at the same time.

"First off, lower your voice. My shawty is resting. You ain't knock or nothing, just strolled up in here like you own the place. Second, bitch, look what time it is, and you just coming to see is she a'ight? What the fuck? She get lunch at three p.m.? Naw, don't even fucking speak. I want your boss in here now. I ain't leaving my angel until I know someone is taking care of her."

"Sir, it is our job to come in here and check on the patient at will without knocking. I am just doing my job," she explained.

"I don't fucking care," I growled. I made sure to say this next part in a lower tone close to this beast's ear. "If you come back around my kid while she is here, they will find you in the Genesee River. Now get the fuck out."

Yeah, her face dropped in shock, and she stopped smacking on that gum and popping those funky lips. Even her red weave seemed to droop as she scurried out of the room like a roach when the light comes on. *That motherfucker better go on and not come back in Kades's room either. She only strolled her ass in here to try to holla at me, not even giving a fuck about her patient.* My name rang bells in these streets, and not for being a lover or even a money nigga. It was because I laid any-one down who stood in my way. I was unbothered and planned to remain that way. I put a smile on my face for Kades and finished enjoying my time with her until she fell asleep.

After having a long talk with the head nurse and slip-ping her a few hundreds to ensure Kades would be good, I decided to go hit the streets and see how my shit was flowing. My phone had been blowing up all day, and the spot on Avenue D was out of everything. I guessed Lox's ass was fucking or something since he didn't respond to that one.

As soon as I pulled up to the trap, this nigga Lamont ran out of the house to meet me.

"Yo, pussy ass, running up to my whip like I'm your bitch or something. Next time wait until I call you or I come inside. I don't date niggas wit' yo' sweet-looking ass, and I don't want anyone making shit hot for me. Fucking idiot."

"Sorry, boss," he replied, but I could see the resentment in his eyes before he turned and walked away. *Yeah, I'ma have to kill this little pretty fucker sooner rather than later.* I spent more time killing niggas than moving these drugs and collecting my money. I didn't understand why no one could just act right. It wasn't hard to do the right thing and just get money. Lamont was going to be the first person on my team I had to get rid of in a long time. Oh, well. I wasn't one of these niggas who felt some way about killing people.

I knew people probably thought I was abused as a child or that I was traumatized or some shit, but no, that wasn't the case, unless you called having two idiots for parents a tragedy. Yep, my dad was in "the home." He wasn't locked up or murdered, and he didn't run away and leave my mom. My parents had been married for thirty years, always worked legit jobs, went to church on Sundays, and appeared to be the perfect loving family. But appearances are just that. What looks like the perfect life is often not at all.

My mom was one of those bitches who just didn't give a fuck, especially when it came to her kids. It wasn't always that way. My pops created that monster. He made her a madwoman who punished at will, and severely. She was angry at him but wouldn't take it up with him, so instead it was taken out on her children. My pops worked at a resort in Montego Bay, Jamaica, while we lived in Kingston. He was a handsome dude like myself, and working on the resort was really no big chore, but he made it seem like it was to make my mom comfortable, even though she had to know in her heart he was lying. He would be gone for five days at a time working double shifts to provide for us and save money to bring everyone to the United States so we could all live the American dream.

Well, along the way of him fulfilling this plan, a lot of shit went left. The good looks he had made all the women love him—tourists, coworkers, locals, and especially his boss. She gave him the best room an employee could hope to have at work: the bedroom in her house.

When I was 6 and my pops had finally saved enough money to make his way to New York and stay with his cousins, we got a big surprise. The week he was supposed to fly out, my dad came strolling through the door with a little girl in his arms. Her name was Azia, and she was the prettiest little girl I had ever seen. She was also my sister. My dad dropped the baby in my mother's lap and told her that Azia's mother didn't want her and had left her at his old job with her papers and a note. So my mom was to take care of her. She cried for months after that and refused to even look at the little girl. So my dad hired a live-in nanny to take care of Azia and help my mom with me.

By the time my sister was old enough to go to school, all of my dad's secrets had come out. He had several kids outside of his and my mom's marriage. He even had a baby in New York with a girl he was living with. That was why he never sent for us to come live there. Baby mamas and outside kids were cropping up like corn on a farm. My mom never said a word to me about it, to anyone actually. I never even heard her cuss at my pops or even cry again. She was like a rock.

As far as everyone in the community knew, Azia was her daughter, but the other kids were treated badly, as were their mothers. See, my mom's older brother, Lennox, also known as Prezi, was an area don, so crossing him was not in anyone's best interest. I never understood why he didn't have my dad killed for cheating on my mother and shaming her with all of these other children. Maybe she asked him not to. Or maybe he just charged it to the game, because it was common where we came from and he was doing the same shit. I think people were only surprised my dad was doing it because he wasn't in the streets. I guess people thought nine-to-five square-ass dudes didn't love lots of bitches too. I can't understand what my mom was going through, because I am a male, and fucking a lot of bitches is in my DNA. But my mom handled this shit all wrong.

Once Azia turned 9, it was like my mom just snapped. We came in from school and did our chores like always.

My mother called Azia into her room, and so it began. She started to punish Azia severely. She first gave away her bed to a neighbor, stating she didn't deserve a bed. I thought my mom had gone crazy. She wasn't thinking about the little red ants that crawled around on the floor. She stopped buying Azia clothes and only bought basic food for her to eat, usually only rice and chicken back. By that time, I was 13 and spent most of my time at my uncle Lennox's house with his son, Lox, so I was eating good every day.

All the money my dad sent my mom she was giving to friends and using to buy clothes for herself and do her hair. She refused to pay us any attention and only did the minimum to keep the house barely running. After a year of this, I was sent home from school because my mother didn't even pay the school fees. Azia was also sent home, but I didn't know this, so I wasn't there to walk her home. As it got later and later and Azia never made it to the house, I was worried.

My mom didn't even get up from her bed, where she was watching movies on her DVD player. My dad would send her the latest bootleg movies when he sent barrels to us. I remember asking her if she was worried about Azia, and she shrugged and turned back to the TV. I wanted to kill her right then. What kind of mother didn't care for her child?

I went to search for my sister and came back with no information at all. Jamaica wasn't like America. You couldn't call the police for a missing child, especially back then. They would just tell you they were filing a report, and nothing ever came of it.

After my uncle put out the word, someone told us she was at Kingston Public Hospital with dog bites all over her body. While she was walking home from school alone, she got lost and was attacked by several stray dogs. My mother never even came to check on her while she was there. After that, my uncle got us visas and sent us to live in New York along with his wife and kids. I was grateful to leave Jamaica because I was worried about my sister. My mom followed us to America, and she moved in with my dad as if their relationship were never interrupted. My pops never said a word to her about how she treated Azia all of the time he was gone. Both of them acted like Azia and I didn't even exist. No holidays were spent with us even though we lived in the same city. There were no phone calls or visits unless my aunt called them or dropped us off at their house.

Well, I never gave a fuck and still didn't. As for my parents, I wasn't close with them. My uncle was all the example I needed, and his wife, Sena, was all the mother we needed. The way my uncle ruled his area in Jamaica was the same way I wanted to run different cities here. He showed Lox and me how not to fear anyone and how to make it clear that everyone around us had to get down or lie down. He was a fair leader, he paid school fees for the kids in the community, and he threw a Christmas party every year where he gave away thousands of dollars in toys and candy to the kids in the area. This was something he still did now, and Lox, Lox's little sister, Kedra, Azia, and I all went home and helped out.

I had a lot of sisters I didn't really know because of my dad's actions. My only brother, Cudjie, well, unfortunately, I did know him. But my sister Azia was my love. I grew up with her. I held her when she cried, and I wondered why my mom hated her. She thought her own mother hated her, never knowing that she wasn't really her mother, which was why she hated her.

We shared a bed when my mom gave hers away, and we both knew neglect at the hand of a mother who just didn't give a fuck. Azia was my heart and soul, and I would have given her anything. I even babysat her bad-ass sons, which was one of the reasons I loved kids so much.

There was something about Inaya that reminded me of my sister, but I guessed I was wrong. I didn't know how to describe what I felt now that I knew Inaya was worthless. I guessed I was just disappointed.

Chapter 5

Inaya

I can't believe this rude-ass nigga. Yeah, I knew that my situation was fucked up, but I was the best mom I could be. I worked a crappy job but stayed looking for a better one. I didn't get any child support even though he assumed I did. Shit, I had to run away from Kadia's father and pray he never found us. I never thought I would leave Noah, let alone run away in terror, but when I thought of the things he had done, I knew I made the only choice I could. *Phantom doesn't know my story. He has no idea what I have been through.*

My mind was all over the place as I tried to focus on the road while driving home from the hospital. I could barely see out of the fucking window while taking home all these fucking toys Phantom bought Kadia today. I went to work for just a few hours, and as soon as I stepped foot in the hospital room, I was greeted by piles of stuff. It looked like the toy aisle from Walmart. The little room was overflowing with roller skates, dolls, a dollhouse, coloring books, and Play-Doh. Oh, and let's not forget the shiny pink Nintendo DS she had been secretly wanting for a long time and the huge teddy bear she was snuggled against in the tiny hospital bed.

The nurse breezed in all smiles. "Her father came by today and spent a few hours with her. They had lunch, and he brought her all of these toys. He even read books to her until she fell asleep." She was happier about the situation than I was.

Even though I shouldn't have been, I was annoyed as hell. Who did he think he was? He just appeared one day and became my enemy but Kadia's knight in shining armor. Maybe I was just annoyed because Phantom didn't want me, and I sure wanted him. Or maybe it just hurt because Kadia would never have a father like him.

Pulling up to the house and realizing I had to carry all this shit in this heat was doing nothing to improve my mood. It took three trips before it was all upstairs and neatly put away in Kadia's room. I was a very neat person, and just because I had no lights or hot water, I still kept the house spotless. As a matter of fact, since she would be home tomorrow, it was a great time to clean the house before the sun went down.

I hurried and began sweeping and running water to mop the downstairs floors. Maybe I would be able to get a good night's sleep tonight because I had a plan for this week that would get my lights back on. This guy I knew, Cudjie, was going to have some weed delivered to my house, and all I had to do was collect the packages and then drive them to Ithaca, which was an hour and a half away. He was paying me $1,000 to make this move for him, and I needed the money so bad I could taste it. *I can turn these lights back on, finally buy toiletries, and even get Kadia some clothes.*

I couldn't have a repeat of what happened to Kadia this week, and I truly had no one to turn to, so I had to figure this out myself. *I won't fail my kid like my mother failed me.* Before I went to lie down, I decided to check my voicemails for the day. My phone didn't get a signal in the hospital.

"Hello, Inaya. This is Mr. Tyler, and I wanted to see if you can come in on Thursday at eight a.m. and do a project involving some of our clients. This is the second part of the job interview. Please call us back and let us know as soon as you can."

I went to bed with a smile on my face after listening to that voicemail. I would be calling first thing in the morning.

The next morning, I was up before the alarm went off on my phone. I was happy I was going to get my baby girl from the hospital today. I walked around my room, humming while pulling my clothes out of the closet. I decided to wear this jean dress I had that flared at the bottom and some gold sandals with gold accessories. Since I couldn't use the flat iron, I used the edge control and some gel to get my long hair under control. I gave myself a middle part and ran the brush through the long, straight tresses. I even took the time to throw some makeup on. As soon as I popped my lips and looked in the mirror, I heard knocking on my door. Shit, I hoped it wasn't someone who wanted to step inside, because I didn't want anyone to know about my situation.

Running down the stairs with my cream and gold MK wristlet in one hand and car keys in the other, I flung the door open. As soon as I did, I could feel my panties getting moist and my heart start to race. There was the man I couldn't get my mind off of. As always, he was greeting me with a frown.

"When is Kadia coming home? I miss my li'l homie," he asked. No hello, not bothering to ask if I was good. I sighed thinking about how good he looked standing there in his light blue Versace jeans and his white V-neck Versace T-shirt. On his feet he had on a pair of white Versace loafers. I wanted to kiss him right on his frowned-up lips.

Instead I just looked down and answered him. "I'm going to pick up Kadia now. I will bring her to say hello if you would like, once we get back here, but only if she is up to it. Also, I didn't get to see you since you visited her yesterday. I really wanted to say thank you for buying all that stuff for Kadia and taking time out to visit with her. It's really all too much, and you didn't have to do any of it."

"Yo, it's cool, ma. I am attached to Kades. She can have anything she wants," he said as he turned to walk away.

"Phantom, I really want to explain all of this to you. I don't want you to think I am a bad mother."

He held up his hand as if he wanted to physically stop me. "Look, I really don't give a fuck what you got to say. There is no excuse, and honestly I don't give a fuck enough about you to pretend I care," he cut me off and walked away.

I could feel the tears begging to leak out of my eyes, but I was determined not to cry. As soon as I sat in the hot-ass car and turned the key, my car made a noise like it was dying and did not start. Banging on the steering wheel, I just put my head down and let those hot-ass tears start to fall. At that moment I just didn't care anymore. I felt so defeated and didn't understand why I kept trying, or why I thought something, anything would change. Now I had to spend my last dollars to take a taxi back from the hospital, because I didn't think Kadia was going to hold up on the bus. Locking up the Maxima, I slowly walked to the bus stop in the front to wait for the next bus.

After half an hour, I could feel my skin burning, and my throat was dry as hell. I still had tears of sadness and frustration running down my cheeks like runaway slaves. An all-black BMW rolled up beside me, and the driver door flew open. I didn't know why he did it, but he came over and sat next to me on the bench. First he handed me an ice-cold bottle of water. Then he pulled me close to him so I could lay my head on his shoulder.

"Come on, ma, don't cry. Let's go get Kades. Worry about the rest later on."

With that being said, Phantom grabbed my hand and led me to the passenger door. *Damn, this car is nice,* I thought as I sank into the peanut butter–colored leather seats. I wondered if I would ever own something this nice as we pulled off. Before I knew it, we were pulling up to the hospital and getting Kadia, then heading back home. The ride both ways was silent. I guessed Phantom wasn't big on talking, or maybe he just didn't want to talk to me. For the first time ever, Kadia was silent in Phantom's presence, due to her being asleep.

"I will carry her in for you. She looks heavy. Plus, you gotta grab the bear and her bag," Phantom demanded as we entered the parking lot. Shit, I wasn't about to argue. Kadia's ass was heavy, and it was hot. He leaned over and grabbed what looked like a gun from his waist and stuck it under the seat of the car. I appreciated that he wouldn't carry my baby with that shit nearby.

Opening the door to my house, I walked him upstairs, where he laid Kadia on her canopy bed. I could see him looking around in every room he went in. He even had the nerve to be wandering around my place while I was making her comfy, running his hands over pictures and shit.

"Damn, Iny, your house is nice as fuck, and clean, too. Hit me if li'l mama needs anything when she wakes up," he commented on his way out.

I can't tell if this jigga is giving me a compliment or a slap in the face.

"What you mean, 'and clean, too'?" I couldn't stop myself from asking.

"Well, you know, ma, you ain't got no lights. Shit, I didn't expect a clean house. I didn't expect furniture, if you want the truth," he spat out just like that.

I wanted to say something else, but the front door had already closed behind him.

Chapter 6

Phantom

Shit, I know I hurt Inaya's feelings when I told her I thought her shit would be dirty, but what the fuck does she expect? Look at how she living without even hot water. I was surprised as hell when I walked through the door. The house smelled like pine cleaner, bleach, and that pink shit you put in the laundry to make the clothes soft, you know, the blue bottle with the teddy bear. She had a wooden bench with wicker baskets in the front hall where she took off her and Kadia's shoes and neatly set them inside. Her living room had a modern-looking couch set in a steel gray with blue and coral accent pillows. She had a large gray carpet covering the floor and pictures to match. On the wall was an okay-size smart TV and one of those $200 surround-sound systems from Walmart.

The kitchen looked just like mine except for the pink, white, and purple everywhere. Shawty even had a pink blender and toaster. Her dining room had a modern square glass table with purple and pink plush chairs and gray placemats. Everything was neat and shining, down to the mirrors she had hanging on the walls. She kicked me out before I could peek in her room and see what her personal space looked like. I was sure it was just as nice as the rest of the house. Shit, even baby girl's room looked like something out of a book. I thought she loved the colors blue and pink, because those colors ruled in her space. Her dresser and chest of drawers even had clear pink and clear blue handles. Looking in her space with the pink fur rug and perfectly made bed made me wonder if I was judging Inaya too much.

I was glad I didn't see Iny's bed, on the real. I was already thinking about fucking her. When she came to the door today in that skimpy jean dress that barely covered her ass, I wanted to bend her over and slide her white lace thong to the side. Yep, her shit was so short I could see the thong she was wearing. She looked sexy as fuck with her long hair straight down her back. It took everything in me not to run my hands through her hair or ask her where the fuck she thought she was going in that little-ass dress. Fuck, now my dick was rock hard thinking about her. I shot a text to the chick I met at Toys "R" Us the other day, Toya. I hoped she was working with something in the bedroom, because if not, she wouldn't last long around me.

Toya hit me back right away like she was waiting next to the phone for me to call. She kept trying to get me to invite her to my place, but I didn't invite these bitches where I lived, especially since I just kept shit casual. They would be stalking me or sleeping outside in their car. My dick game was that good. Then you got the women who steal, and I didn't want to have to push back a bitch's wig for having sticky fingers.

As soon as I saw the address, I knew to take my Audi. I wasn't taking my Bentley to the projects where she lived. I pulled onto Waring Road and prayed she didn't have roaches or anything. *I should just take ma to a hotel. This area is all hoodrats and rats.*

"Yo, I'm outside. Come open up the door," I told Toya as I stood outside her door looking at all the young boys playing dice and arguing in the pissy-ass hallway. I saw some bags with flashes of light blue on them changing hands. Well, damn, my shit was everywhere in these streets. I wasn't even mad at 'em.

"Hey, baby. I am so glad you came to see me," she said with a big-ass grin on her face and a $5 "silk" robe on, leaving little for me to imagine.

As soon as I stepped in the house, I wanted to walk back out again. I didn't see any roaches, but the couches looked gray/brown. Couldn't tell if it was the color or from dirt, but I wasn't taking any chances. Her tiny kitchen had dishes piled up and falling onto the counter. The trash was falling on the floor, and the floor itself looked like it wasn't safe to walk on. My Versace shoes were sticking to the cheap linoleum, and I was just praying nothing would be stuck to the bottom and come home with me.

"Mommy, I'm hungry, and the baby needs to be changed," a little girl about 7 came out, talking to Toya. The poor kid looked like she hadn't seen a bath in a while, and her hair was damaged and not combed at all. When she looked up at me, she didn't even acknowledge my presence. She looked right past me like I wasn't even in the room. Yeah, her mama was a ho, because she looked like having men in her space was a regular thing. Toya and I were definitely not going to work out.

"Toya, it's cool, ma. I ain't know you had your shorties in here. I can come check you later." I tried to get the fuck out of her space, but she waved me off.

"Don't worry about them. They good. Let's go to my room. I promise it's nicer than out here. These kids tear up everything. Lalani, go have a seat until my company leaves. You know better," she yelled at the annoyed-look-ing child.

As I walked around her and past the living room, I could see a baby and a small boy no older than 3 sitting on a bed with no sheet. Damn, this bitch was wicked. She needed to take care of her fucking kids. I didn't even feel comfortable smashing with her li'l ones almost in the same room. This small-ass apartment left nothing to the imagination, and I knew they could hear everything through the paper-thin walls.

As soon as we stepped in her bedroom, it was a little bit better. The bed had a cheap comforter set from Walmart and what looked like clean sheets. She had a dresser with a TV on top and had the nerve to have some candles lit like she was setting the scene up for some romantic shit.

"Come on, babe. Lie on the bed, and make yourself at home," she said as she dropped her robe and stood back. Carefully sitting on the edge of the bed, I dropped my pants and boxers while motioning for her to come closer. As soon as she got close enough, I grabbed her head and shoved her mouth toward my dick. She was slobbering and sucking like a hose on a vacuum cleaner the minute her mouth connected.

"Yes, bitch, suck the skin offa my shit. Don't stop, Toya." I couldn't even tell if she was doing a good job or if I was just turned on because Inaya's fat ass was on my mind. I could feel myself getting ready to nut. She was playing with her pussy, and cum was running down her fingers. Shoving my dick way in the back of her throat and grabbing her blond weave, I let loose.

"Make sure you swallow, too," I demanded, making sure all of my seeds hit her taste buds. She was licking that shit up like she loved it.

While she was lying back and opening up those legs, hoping for some of my thick, curved dick, I was pulling my pants up and getting ready to go.

"Umm, Phantom, where are you going? We ain't even fuck or nothing," she asked with her mouth turned up into a little pout.

For effect, I checked my watch, then looked back at shawty. "Hey, ma, I have a run to make. I was just trying to stop by real quick and see what you up to and all. By the way, thanks for the nut. You know how to make a nigga feel good."

"Well, come and see me later after you handle your business, all right, Phantom? Maybe you can bring your little girl by, and she can play with my kids."

"Yeah, we will see. I'ma hit you later," I said as I hurried and got in my whip. Fuck no, Kades couldn't come over to this dirty-ass apartment. Well, damn, these hoes were something else. I wondered where those kids' daddies were, because Toya's ass was truly living foul. She wanted me to lie up and fuck her all day while the kids were in the room next to us, hungry, dirty, and listening to all of that shit. Plus, she'd told me she was only 22. *How she got three kids already?* I bet the pussy was all out of shape and wasn't worth my time.

I'm not even knocking ma because she got so many kids or she living in the PJs. She could clean up the crib and be a better parent. There are no excuses. This was why I didn't mess with any female with kids, because they didn't take care of them the way I thought they should. All I could think about was Iny. Even though her situation was messed up, she didn't stop taking care of baby girl. Her hair was always done, she was always clean, and her school uniforms were always fresh. I wondered if I should listen to her and hear what she had to say. I didn't want to get attached to her because I didn't want to find out she was truly like every other girl I knew. I didn't want to get hurt.

As soon as I came in the crib, I told Lox about a new bitch I was fucking and how she was dirty as hell. He laughed so hard I thought he was going to piss himself.

"Yo, nigga, I am glad you think I am a fucking joke, man. I don't know where I be finding these bitches at. It's like I got a sign on my head inviting all ratchet, no-good, and scandalous bitches to me," I shot at him while walking back outside.

I'd forgotten one of my phones in the car, and I needed to make a call. As soon as I walked outside, I saw the manager lurking around Iny's door. What the fuck did she want? Her old penguin-looking ass was peeking in the windows and shit like the police. Before she left, I peeped her shoving a white envelope between the cracks of the door.

As soon as she rounded the corner, I snatched that shit up to read it. I hoped like hell Inaya was at least paying the fucking rent, because this screamed of an eviction notice.

> *Attention Tenant in 733 Passava Lane,*
> *It has been brought to our attention that you are residing in this unit with no active electricity. This is a violation of your lease per Section 5.1, and if you do not restore the services within forty-eight hours, you will be served an eviction notice and have seven days to vacate the property. All deposits will be forfeited with the eviction and termination of your lease.*
> *Thank You,*
> *Management*

I didn't know why, but I snatched the letter and shoved it in my pocket before I went in the crib. I decided to text this chick I knew at the gas and electric company to see if she was working today. As soon as she said she was, I made my way down there.

"Yo, ma, I need to pay on my cousin's light bill. She got a little one who is sick in the hospital, so I want to look out for her." I couldn't tell shorty it was a chick I wanted to fuck, or she would act a whole fool.

"All right, Phantom, I can help you, but when we gonna hang out again? I miss the way your dick feels in the back of my throat. I love tasting that thick cum. It tastes like a milkshake." She kept talking shit while her hand crept under the desk and onto my jeans. Her hands brought my man to life, but I was not a fan of the thot shit. I mean, this bitch was at work, talking loud as fuck about sucking my dick, and was damn near trying to rape me in front of her boss, customers, and everybody else in the RG&E office.

"A'ight, Shena. We gonna chill this weekend, girl. Just hit me up. What's the balance on her bill?" I asked while giving her a smile that made my dimple pop out. I didn't smile much, but I wanted to get her in the right mindset to give me what I wanted.

"Five hundred sixty-eight dollars is past due and must be paid in full in order for us to restore the service."

"Cool. Put this on the bill, and if you see this shit get behind again, hit me up and let me know so I can take care of it before it gets cut off. Her little girl has a serious asthma issue and can't be without electricity," I explained, handing her $1,500 in cash. "This for you. I appreciate you helping me out on this one." I handed her a few hundred and got up to go.

"Thanks, Phantom. Let her know the service will be on in the morning. I moved it up to the top of our list," she replied, winking and licking her lips.

I hit her with a head nod and kept it moving. I couldn't wait to get back to the house and see if Kades was up yet. I stopped and picked her up some roses and some candy. Shit, I figured all kids liked candy, and I would do anything to bring a smile to baby girl's face.

Chapter 7

Inaya

Even though it was a Saturday, I was up super early. My grandma convinced my mom she needed Kadia with her this weekend because of how she almost died in the hospital, and my mom even seemed like she cared and agreed that Kadia should come over so they could spoil her. I didn't believe shit my mother said, but I knew my grandmother would take good care of her.

Today was the big day. The packages I was collecting from Cudjie should be delivered before noon so I could get on the road and make this two-hour drive for the drop-off. I could feel my stomach twisting in knots as I ran into the bathroom and got sick. I never wanted to involve myself in illegal dealings again, especially now that I had Kadia. All I could think about was that if something happened to me, what would happen to her? We didn't really have anybody, and my mom wouldn't take care of her even if I were dead, surely not if I went to jail. But I was determined that my baby was coming home to lights on in this house on Monday no matter what.

After checking my phone for what seemed like the hundredth time and lying on my bed for a few hours listening for the mailman to knock on my door in the silence of the house, I decided to go downstairs. I guessed it was out of habit or something, but I hit the light switch on

the way down the stairs, and the lights popped on. *Wait?
What the hell?* How did I have lights? Running into the
kitchen, I could see the microwave and stove had random
numbers blinking where the time should be. Opening
the empty fridge, I heard the whirring of the freezer
struggling to get cold again. I found the latest past due
notice to call and check my balance, and my hand shook
while holding the bill. I was sure this was some mistake,
because I had not made a payment yet. As soon as I heard
them say I had a credit of $932, I felt like I was being
tricked. *How did this happen?* I wondered if they applied
a credit from another person's account to mine accidently.
Those things happened, I was sure. At the day care once
we mixed up parents' payments for a few months before
the parent actually making the payments complained.
Maybe whoever it was had an account number close to
mine. As soon as I finished this run, I was still going
to take them the money I needed to pay.

Before I could focus on this blessing, or mistake, the
mailman was knocking at my door. "Hello, miss, I have
packages here for Sara Jenkins. I need a signature," he
said while handing me an electronic tablet-looking thing.
I was nervous, but he looked bored as hell. I signed the
name Sara Jenkins and watched him pile a total of eight
boxes at my doorstep and stroll away. I texted Cudjie,
letting him know the stuff was here, and waited for him
and his partner to show up.

I was a little pissed because he'd said *a* package, not
eight. This would look crazy to anyone watching. It
seemed like Cudjie was careless, and I wasn't trying to
get caught up.

Before I knew it, they were at the house and had
unpacked the neatly packaged bricks of weed and placed
them in several shopping bags. I guessed that was how I
was driving them, but this didn't seem real smart. If I got

pulled over, I wouldn't have a chance. Now my belly was really sick, and I didn't think this was such a good idea. As Cudjie put the last bag in the car, I heard a familiar voice.

"Yo, son, what you doing out this way?" Phantom questioned Cudjie.

Shit, I hoped he wasn't trying to start no bullshit and mess this up for me. I couldn't hear all they were saying, but Phantom seemed to be yelling at him. Before I could blink, the car door I was sitting next to was yanked open, and I was being snatched out by Phantom's strong hand.

"Yo, ma, this shit right here is not for you. I don't know why you always doing dumb shit that can fuck up Kadia's life. Your mama drop you on ya fucking head or something? Go take your ass in the house now, and I don't want to catch you talking to this nigga again," he shouted at me while shoving me toward the crib. I was crying even though I wasn't sad. I was angry.

Who the hell did Phantom think he was to tell me I was dumb or making stupid decisions? He had no idea how much I needed this money. *First, this motherfucker tells me I'm a terrible mother for not having any lights on, and then he ruins my only chance to keep these fucking lights on for my baby.* Cudjie gave me half the money when the packages arrived safely, but it still wouldn't give me enough to do anything extra I had planned on doing for Kadia or getting the new battery for my car that it needed to start. I could hear Cudjie apologize, laugh, and call Phantom boss as he got in the car and drove away.

"Yo, I am trying to talk to you, and you still walking." He ran up on me and snatched my arm so I was facing him. Cutting my eyes, I began losing it and yelling at him.

"Look, Jahdair, you can call me a bad mother, or a waste girl or careless or even a bitch, I don't care. You don't know what my story is or what I am going through, and you clearly cannot respect me trying to straighten shit out for Kadia so she never has to go without the comforts of electricity again. I'm a single mother, there is no child support, and Kadia's father isn't someone who can be around her. I don't make a ton of money, but I look for new and better jobs every day, and every day I get up and take my ass to the crappy job I do have and give it a hunnit while I am there. I am not lazy or dirty, and I don't deserve the way you talk down to me every time you see me. I go without getting my hair and my nails done to make sure I pay for extras at Kadia's private school like violin lessons and ballet classes. Yes, she gets a scholarship, but that stuff is not included, and neither are her uniforms or shoes. I'm not perfect, but I am trying my best, and I like you, I do. I think you are sexy and loving toward Kadia, but you deal wit' me like shit, and I want you to stay away from me!" I shouted as I stormed in my house and slammed the door in his face.

After trying to call Cudjie a few times with no response, I decided to have AAA jump my car so I could go to AutoZone and get a battery. The gas and electric company said I had a credit, so until they found the glitch, I had to make this money work out. Walking to the car so I could wait, I was happy I didn't run into Jahdair, because I meant what I said. I had been put down in the past, and I couldn't do it anymore.

Once I was jumped and made my way to AutoZone for a new battery, I was left with $450 of Cudjie's money and $80 from my paycheck. I also had $195 saved, which I was putting away to pay the light bill. I'd keep that in savings though. I decided to head to Walmart and get food and some household items.

An hour later I had a cart loaded with all of my baby's favorite foods and snacks as well as meat, sides, fruits, milk, and cereals. I also stocked up on Gain laundry detergent, Snuggle, paper towels, and toilet paper. I was feeling so happy. No more cold baths or eating food from a corner store microwave every day. As a treat, I got Kadia some Doc McStuffins bubble bath and a Spinbrush toothbrush, the one you could put stickers on and decorate yourself. This shit always happens in Walmart. I ended up with stuff I never came in there for.

After loading up the trunk with all of my purchases, I made my way down the street to The Marketplace Mall. First I stopped in Rainbow. I hoped they were having an end-of-season sale so I could grab my baby some clothes. Today was my lucky day as I saw racks and racks of $5 and $10 outfits from Juicy Couture and Rocawear. They had some cute $3 dresses and bright-colored shirts. Making my way to Macy's, next I picked her up two polo outfits that were on clearance, and then I hit Jimmy Jazz. My arm was starting to hurt carrying all this stuff by the time I got in the store, and if Kadia had shoes at home that didn't hurt her feet, I would have turned around and headed for the car. I didn't know how my cousin Sahnai did it. She shopped like it was an Olympic sport.

As soon as I began looking at the prices on the sneakers, praying I could find something cute for under $40, I felt a pair of eyes on me. I looked around, but I didn't see anyone who looked familiar, so I shrugged it off. Not seeing anything in my price range, I dropped my head and began to slowly make my way out of the store. I would return some of the clothes and come back for the shoes. She needed them more.

"Hey, ma, wait. You're Inaya, right?" asked a tall brown-skinned guy with shoulder-length dreads. He had some weird greenish eyes and full lips he kept licking. I thought it was more out of habit than him trying to look sexy. He was sexy but not my type. Lately my only type was Phantom. He did look familiar though.

"I'm sorry. Do I know you or something?" I asked, looking at him suspiciously.

"I'm Phantom's cousin. I have seen you, but we were not introduced. My name is Lox. Are you okay? You seem kind of down."

"Look, I don't want to be rude, but I don't want anything to do with Jahdair or Phantom or whatever he wants to call himself or anyone who has anything to do with him. I am okay. Thank you for asking," I spat out while continuing on my way to the exit.

Laughing, he replied, "Yeah, Phantom has that effect on all the ladies. I won't apologize for him, but I will tell you he is feeling you. I know he has a fucked-up way of showing it, but it's true. Usually a female won't even hold his attention for more than a week, but you, well, you still holding on. Ma, I can tell you not doing all right. I heard about what happened today wit' that nigga Cudjie, and, li'l sis, let me tell you, he is trouble. Not even worth it. So come on and tell me what size shoes my li'l homie Kades wear so we can sort her out."

Damn, Lox was so nice. I was also embarrassed that it was so obvious I couldn't afford shoes for my daughter. He was respectful and didn't make me feel bad about the situation. I wished I'd met him first and that he was the man my heart and body craved.

"Thanks, Lox. I will pay you back as soon as I can. She wears a size 10. We can just get her one pair, and she will be good."

I guessed Lox had fallen in love with Kadia too, because I left Jimmy Jazz with six new pairs of sneakers for her, Nike socks, and even a few track suits. Lox walked me to the car and carried my bags after making sure Kadia had all she needed.

"Look, Inaya, even though I don't know you well, I can see you truly are a good girl. I know shit seems rough for now, but just keep on trying. I know you mad at Phantom, but he will come around, and once he does, just welcome him in. Don't give up on him. He could be the one for you. Don't miss your Prince Charming, girl." He laughed at himself. That shit did make me laugh a little.

Once I got home and started unpacking everything and putting everything away, the groceries first, I thought about what Lox said. I feel like God puts people in our lives for a reason. I wished I could figure out the reason he brought me Jahdair. I didn't want to be surprised again or hurt, and I didn't want to ruin Kadia's bond with him. I didn't know what I wanted or what I should do.

Putting away my baby's clothes, I smiled to myself. She was going to be so happy when she saw all the new, pretty stuff, especially the white and pink Jordans that came out today. Taking the boxes out of the bag, I noticed money in the bottom of the last one. Counting out $800, I could feel tears well up in my eyes. Lox was good people. He didn't have to buy Kadia shit, and then he was nice enough to sneak and give me some money.

I lay down and dialed my cousin Sahnai. We talked about her moving back to Rochester because DC was too expensive, and we made plans for her and her son, Q, to stay with me until she found a place. Knowing her it would be no time before some man came to her rescue and bought her spoiled ass a crib or whatever. I didn't mean it in a bad way. I never hated on Sah. She did things her way, and I did things mine. As I snuggled into my pillow, I couldn't help the smile that went all the way to my heart. I couldn't wait to see my cousin.

Chapter 8

Lox

Seeing Inaya in the mall today looking like she wanted to cry made my heart go out to her. You could tell she wanted to get her shorty some shoes but couldn't afford them. I wasn't Captain Save-a-ho, but I decided to help her out. Anyway, I felt like she was going to be Phantom's first girlfriend, first love. I thought she had what it took to reach his heart. I could see it when he looked at her. Plus, a nigga never talked about just smashing her or making her give him head. That whole speech about how he didn't fuck bad mothers was a lie.

Most times the nigga didn't know if these bitches had kids and sure as hell didn't give a fuck about their situations. I was no doctor or anything, but between his mama and his sick-ass baby's mom, his heart had to be ice cold and his mentality toward women totally fucked up. Hell, that mess his baby's mom did even fucked my head up. I started to look at females with a lot more distrust than before.

Lennox Qualyl Hall III, better known as Lox, my name should have been the one ringing bells in these streets instead of Phantom's, but his viciousness did enough for the whole family. Phantom was my first cousin on his mom's side and my dad's. My father, the infamous don named Prezi, best known for the murder of some high-level politicians in the . . . well, I won't get into what party they were in, but it was a gruesome sight. I loved my dad, even though he was a killer. He gave my mom a lot of love. He cheated here and there and even had a few kids other than my sister and me in the earlier years, but he never let that shit reach my mom. No women ever called her phone or came to our home. He never put any other female above her, and to this day they were still going strong.

I didn't try to be my pops at all. I was just as ruthless as him and Phantom. I didn't mind killing if I had to, and some days I craved it. I just was more low-key with my temper. Pushing drugs to people didn't move me one bit. I wanted to feel sorry when I saw people walking around high and sleeping outside because all their money went to feed their addiction, but I just didn't. I wasn't like my dad. I wasn't worried about taking care of the community or being a people person. I was happy with who I was. I felt like in this world you have to fight to get what you want. If you are weak, you are just weak, and that's it.

One thing I wasn't was a man whore. Yeah, I fucked bitches. I mean, come on, I had peanut butter brown skin, sexy green eyes, and the body of an Adonis. I had had a few girlfriends, a few baby mama scares, and even some stalker chicks. Okay, some real live stalker chicks. I was even kidnapped by one of 'em.

She was this white girl I met at the grocery store. I mean, for a white girl she was stacked, ass was fat, breasts sitting up high. I fucked with Jane for a while because she didn't need shit from a nigga. She lived in the 'burbs, owned her own salon, and didn't need my money. It was actually a relief to mess with someone like her. I made it clear I wasn't into settling down, but we could be casual, fuck, go on a few dinners, or catch a movie here and there. I wasn't a mean nigga like my cousin. I respected women for the most part.

One day while walking through the mall with my new friend Cari, we ran right into Jane. Jane's face got red, and she began creating a scene. Now I am not one for a scene, and to give Cari credit, she tried to just walk away, but Jane started swinging on her, not really hitting much but not letting her walk away. Before I knew it, Jane was in the fountain with blood everywhere. I walked with my gun on me at all times, so I grabbed Cari and got the fuck out of there before a fight turned into a police shoot-out.

Everything seemed cool after that. Jane even apologized to me and offered to make me dinner and give me a massage to make it up to a nigga. Now this was where I should have run, but I had no idea what was coming. I really thought it was not a big thing to her since she had let it go. The night I went over to chill after a nice meal of salmon and rice, she laid me down on her king-size bed and used some scented oil to massage my back. Before I knew it, I was waking up in her bed handcuffed and tied to the posts with rope. The door was closed and locked. She had slipped something in my drink, and she held me for over a week, having sex with me as much as she physically could in that time frame until Phantom figured her out and rescued me.

The whole time she was mumbling about how no one but she would get my big black dick and she was never letting me go. I felt like I was in *Fatal Attraction* or one of those Lifetime movies chicks be watching. Thinking back on it now, it was funny. Shit, that was what I got for fucking with a white chick anyway. Look at the movies. Their asses aren't stable.

I thought honestly I just hadn't settled down because I hadn't found the right one. I mean, the one who touched my heart and who consumed my mind, my body, and my soul. Well, if I was being honest with myself, I did find the right one, but somehow she got away. I thought about

Sahnai all the time. She was the only girl I ever made love to instead of fucked, cooked for, took shopping, held hands with, and opened up to. Sahnai and I were best friends first, and then we started having sex. Even so, we never made us official, and once I decided it should have been done a long time before, she was gone. Just up and moved, changed her phone number, the works.

Damn, man, I missed her. She was so pretty, her brown skin was flawless, and her light brown eyes were so full of life. She wanted to be an accountant. I remembered her always messing with numbers and asking us these crazy-ass questions like, if a train was going twenty miles an hour, how many miles would it travel in a year? I used to hit her with the blank stare until she rolled her little almond-shaped eyes and stomped her feet. She would say she was mad I wasn't even trying. I would kiss her until she laughed and kissed me back.

Sahnai was life. She could do it all—keep her crib and mine clean, cook, and she could slay some hair. She would retwist my dreads and even braid Phantom's hair. Honestly, I was hoping she would give me a few kids. I even thought she was pregnant right before she left. She was sleeping all day and throwing up everywhere, even craving strange shit like peanut butter and banana on toast.

One day, I went to pick her up from the salon she worked in so she didn't have to take the train, only for the owner to tell me Sahnai had moved away and wasn't coming back. Just like that she was gone. Her number had been disconnected, and her place was for rent. If it weren't for her old employer telling me she had moved, I would have been worried she was dead. At first I was worried someone got to her, one of my enemies or a random crazy.

I waited for months, hoping she was just going through something or that she had a family emergency and would call me with an apology or an "I love you," but that day never came. In the back of my mind, I knew it had something to do with me, but I didn't know what. I even felt like my mom knew what was up because she never spoke badly about Sahnai, and when I cried on her shoulder, she would look at me and just shake her head. When Phantom would call her a bitch and a thot, my mom would smack him upside his head and tell him he knew better. I swore she was the only one who could hit that psycho nigga, because he had no problem hitting women back.

Anyway, I didn't let that shit turn my heart cold. We were young, and I still believed I could find the one worth settling down with.

"Yo, Lox, what you doing up there? You gonna roll wit' me to this party on Friday at Euphoria?" Phantom asked, barging into my room and interrupting my thoughts.

"Ol' big-head-ass nigga, you don't know how to knock or nothing? You know I hate going to that small-ass club. If something ever goes down in that bitch, we gonna have to kill everything moving just to get to the one door," I said, stating straight facts. That fucking place was a death trap.

"Nigga, you going, so stop whining and shit. Maybe you can meet your future wifey while we are there," he laughed while walking out of the room.

"Hey yo, fuck you!" I yelled after him. He was an ass-hole sometimes, but that was still my nigga, more like a brother than a cousin.

Chapter 9

Phantom

Here we go again. The fucking girl next door got my blood boiling. Of all the people she had to link up with, it would be my snake-ass half brother Cudjie. I wondered where she even met a nigga like him. I swore he acted just like my pops except he was some wannabe king of New York. He rode off my name and even threw around my uncle's name sometimes to seem like he was someone of importance or someone to be afraid of when, on the real, he wasn't shit. Cudjie and I were only a few years apart. I was 25 and he was 22. He looked just like our pops: brown skin, raggedy Brillo pad–looking hair in a low cut. He needed to go bald, because that shit made him look homeless. We all had the same black eyes, but his and our dad's were beady, like a rat. I wished being young was the only reason he was an idiot, but having met his mother, it seemed to be a genetic trait.

What was Iny thinking, about to drive out of town with all those pounds of weed in the car like that? Shit wasn't even hidden away and couldn't all fit in the trunk. They had Macy's shopping bags filled with the weed sitting on the back seats chilling like she was about to drive around loaves of bread or some other legal shit. I knew how Cudjie was. His ass was careless when it came to his hustle. And anything I gave him to flip or sell I didn't even look for a fast return on because he always fucked up something first. He was like a tornado. He took down everything in his path. Lox and I really didn't supply him anymore because of his shaky payment history. I would have killed him, but my uncle told me God wouldn't like it if I killed my only brother. So out of respect for Lennox, he was still walking around, for now.

I honestly didn't know whose shit he was collecting next door to my crib, but it wasn't mine. We didn't deliver the way these came in, sloppy and shit. Not a chance in hell. All my shit was driven in from out of town. It was taken off the boats in NYC or Miami and then driven up by the trucker boys I had on my payroll. This having the post office deliver drugs to a chick's house was an amateur move. I knew he knew better, but that's what I mean about him. If shit went left, Iny would have been caught up, and he would have been walking around free and clear. I had seen him do it before. His own baby's mom had their daughter in jail because he allowed her to get caught collecting a box filled with drugs. Worst thing was he put the package in her legal name, she signed and collected it, and a few minutes after she closed the door, that bitch was being kicked off the hinges by the narcotics division.

The saddest part was she had no idea drugs were in the box. He set her up, and when she was locked up, he moved on to the next chick like she never existed. I felt so bad I got li'l mama a good lawyer, and after ten months she got out with probation. I did it for my niece. I didn't want her father's fucked-up ways to ruin her whole life before she even had a chance.

I knew this nigga was being funny collecting drugs next to the spot I lay my head at. I was a low-key type of person, and not too many people knew where I was, but I knew he did. He was supposed to be family, but this nigga's definition of family was out of a dictionary I'd never read.

Man, I fucked up with Inaya again. I didn't know what it was about her, but I wanted her to be perfect, and she wasn't, and it pissed me off. Every time I saw her, I wanted to kiss her and strangle her at the same damn time. Now she was really pissed off with me, and I hoped she didn't try to keep Kadia away from me. Shit, I just hoped she talked to me again, because I was being way too hard on her. I never thought about how hard all this shit was on her.

Being broke sucks, and being a single mom is hard as fuck. My sister Azia was a single mom, and even though she didn't want for anything financially because I got her, and the boys had me and Lox as role models, I remembered her once telling me that the hardest part of being a single mom was not having that support system. She said it was hard wanting someone to look to for decisions on the home and the boys, wanting someone to help when they were sick or had activities, or just needing someone there to hold her at the end of the day, someone to be there so she wasn't lonely anymore.

My sister's boyfriend was a good dude. I never thought I would be okay with my baby sister having a boyfriend at all, but he went to school, had a good job, and treated her right. It wasn't his fault she was left alone. It was just his time. Jason was a firefighter, and he died in a fire after saving a little girl who was trapped on the third floor.

I could understand how little sis could feel lonely. I wondered if Inaya felt that way. But she was right. I didn't know her story at all. Kadia's father could have been in jail, or dead, or just a deadbeat. I never even took the time to get to know Iny. I didn't even know how old she was, or what her goals were, or her favorite foods. I knew she went to school, but I didn't know for what. I could have told her, "Good job," on keeping her head up and still going to class even when shit got rough. Damn, I needed to talk to her, but I was not used to being rejected, and she was definitely not feeling the kid last night.

I was not the type of nigga to apologize, but I was going to head over to her crib and see if she was okay. *Checking on her should let her know how I feel. Iny is different.* Most females didn't care how I talked to them or treated them as long as I fucked them good or let them spend my money. Shit, with all Iny had going on, she had never asked me for a penny.

As soon as I raised my hand to knock on the door, I noticed the keys dangling from the lock. Damn, I wondered if she knew how dangerous that shit was. I mean, yeah, we lived in a good neighborhood, but not in a good world. Especially after today with shady-ass Cudjie knowing where she laid her head and her messing up his plans. He could have come back at any time. He didn't care who he hurt when he got mad. He whooped his own mother's ass if she told him no. Turning the keys to unlock the door, I knocked slightly to let her know I was coming in, but when she didn't answer I just let myself in.

Slowly walking up the stairs, I went to the master bedroom. I could hear the TV on. It must have been some comedy, because every few seconds I could hear the background laughter from the audience. Today the house smelled like flowers and some kind of food. It smelled good. It made my stomach rumble, and I remembered I didn't eat dinner.

"Iny," I called out, but she never even budged in her sleep. All she had on was a pair of cheetah-print panties, and she was sleeping with her little butt in the air. She was curled up with a pillow, and her hair was spread out on another. I could still see the tearstains on her cheeks from her crying. Damn, I felt bad because I knew I caused those tears.

Taking off my shoes and jeans, I slowly slid onto the bed. I shook her a little, and she jumped up out of her sleep.

"What the hell are you doing in my house . . . wait, in my bed? Who let you in? I meant it, Phantom. I never want to see you again," she screamed. Sitting up in bed, she looked down and realized I could see her breasts. They were perfect. I wanted to lick around the brown nipple and make her scream. I had to move and adjust my dick because, like always, when I was around Inaya my man was rock hard.

She pulled the sheet up and pointed to the door. "Get out. But not before you tell me how you got in."

"Inaya, you left the keys in the front door. I knocked when I walked in and called your name once I hit your bedroom door, but you didn't move an inch."

She just sat there with her head tilted to the side like she was waiting for something else. *What the fuck she waiting on?* I gave all the explanation I had.

"Yo, ma, what you waiting on? Fix your fucking head, or it's gonna drop off your shoulder and roll out the door."

"Yeah, nigga, I'm waiting on you to tell me how I am a fucking dummy for leaving my keys in the door or some other rude-ass comment. Oh, and I am waiting on you to put your clothes on that you have laid over my white chair and bounce," she said, straightening her head out and lying back on her fluffy pillows.

Getting under the covers and grabbing the remote control, I pulled her a little closer so I could whisper in her ear.

"Inaya, I am sorry. I am too rough on you, but I need you to make better choices, babes."

She looked up at me with her dreamy brown eyes, and I wanted so badly to kiss her lips, but kissing bitches was not something I was in to. Shit, she could have had those lips on my brother's dick for all I knew.

"So what we watching? Because this girly shit you got on ain't gonna work," I said while flipping through the channels. We decided on the new season of *X-Files*, and before I knew it, she was sleeping like a baby in my arms. I had never cuddled in bed with any woman, not even Shawnie. The last girl who laid they ass near me in a bed and watched TV was Azia.

There's something about her I have to get out of my system. Before I could stop myself, I ran my fingers along her thighs then up to her nipples.

"Ahhh," she moaned in her sleep.

I could feel the pre-cum dripping down my leg already, and I knew I had to feel inside of her. Dipping my finger in her panties and touching her clit, I felt she was dripping wet. Rolling her over and laying my body on top of her, I began kissing her neck. I rubbed the head of my dick against her panties, then moved them to the side as her hand grabbed him and began rubbing him against her pussy. I felt like I was going to die it felt so good. Not even thinking about a condom or babies, I slid inside and found the tightest pum pum I had ever been in.

We had sex for over an hour. Once I had her face-down and she started rubbing her clit while I was deep inside, I knew I wasn't going to make it much longer.

"Yes, Iny, cum for me, baby. Just like that. Don't stop playing wit' that pussy."

"Jahdair, fuck me harder, baby. Yessss."

We came at the same time, and she snuggled her sweaty body up to mine and started snoring. Smoothing her hair out of her eyes, I couldn't help but lean down and lightly kiss her lips.

Before the sun came up, I snuck out of her embrace and threw on my clothes so I could get out of there before morning. Throwing a few stacks on the bedside table so she and Kades had some spending money, or whatever she may have needed to do with it, I lightly closed the door, hearing it click behind me. I wasn't sneaking out because li'l ma felt like just a fuck. I just didn't want Kadia to find me in her mama's bed first thing in the morning. *I respect them too much for that,* I said to myself as I undressed again in my room and hit my king-size bed hard.

Chapter 10

Sahnai

I could feel the difference as soon as my BMW hit the raggedy-ass roads in Rochester, New York. I wondered what I was doing here. Yeah, there were some money niggas, but not like when I was in DC. Plus, I probably ran through everyone's pockets who was worth anything. Although I couldn't wait to meet this new guy who had my cousin all in her feelings. Shit, Naya was avoiding niggas like they all got AIDS or something ever since her ex. I couldn't blame her. I would not let another man into my and my daughter's personal space after everything that sick nigga Noah did to her and Kadia.

Anyway, tall, dark, and rich was just how I liked them, and Phantom sounded like he fit the bill. I was sure he had a friend or a cousin, maybe even a brother, who had the same profile I could sink my claws into.

I guessed a part of me just missed my cousin. Inaya and I were raised together by our grandmother. Shit, I missed my grandmother, too. She was our rock coming up. I was such a handful I honestly didn't know why she even kept me around. I was angry at the whole world, and I showed it in every way possible: skipping school, fighting the teachers, and I would even act out at church. I locked the Sunday school teacher in a utility closet and taught the other kids how to gamble by playing cards and shooting dice. All of that acting out was a waste of my time and energy. I was hoping my mother would come and love me more than her addiction. Little did I know it was already too late. She had died of a heroin overdose when I was 10, and none of us even knew until years later.

When Grams was diagnosed with ovarian cancer, I finally slowed down. Seeing her sick from the chemo treatments and not even able to get out of bed some days really hit me hard. I remembered feeling so guilty about all I had put her through. I thought about killing myself. I felt like I didn't appreciate all that she did to take care of Inaya and me and like I took her for granted. She taught me how to love selflessly. I was happy I didn't take the easy way out because it would have hurt the people who loved me, and I wouldn't have been there when Grams needed me.

Those days were rough, but at the age of 15, I learned about the power of a pretty face and a tight waist. When Grams got sick, she couldn't work as a nurse anymore, and the way the system worked, it could be months before you even got your first disability check. This was when Naya and I learned about suffering. Sad thing was Naya never learned another way, while I was determined to never miss another meal, to never waste time with someone who wasn't taking care of me.

While Inaya was running drugs for the local dope boys, I was flaunting my pretty looks and hot body, making sure those same dope boys were taking care of me financially. Don't get it twisted, I wasn't a ho or easy. I didn't fuck these guys. I guess my cute face just made those niggas want to throw their dough my way. And thank God they did. That was how we survived until Grams got better. Shit, that was how I survived my whole life. Except when I was with Lox. I never had to use men to survive when I was with him.

Pulling up to the address Naya gave me and driving into her parking lot, I could see she was in a good area. I was happy for her even though I knew something was up. We barely talked over the last few months. She was always saying her phone battery was messing up, and her voice was filled with stress. Shit, we talked more when she lived in Toronto with that devil Noah. She wouldn't even let me talk to Kadia anymore. Every time she had some excuse. Kadia was sleeping or in school or outside playing. Playing with whom? I knew she wasn't letting my 4-year-old cousin outside to play alone. *She isn't slick.*

Looking in the rearview mirror, I watched the best thing in my life sleep. He was slumped over in his car seat with his iPad in his lap and his *Cars* headphones sliding off of his head. His dreads were falling over his eyes, and the sweat was dripping off his perfect eyelashes. Sometimes I thought he knew when I was watching him, because he smiled in his sleep.

"Q, wake up, baby. We are at cousin Naya's house. Come on, my sweet boy." I coaxed him to wake up as he opened one of his little green eyes to glare at me. My baby hated being woken up. Just like his father. *The father he will never know.*

Checking myself out in the visor mirror, I took the brush I kept in the car along with my emergency gel and smoothed the back of my short hairstyle down. Touching my fingertips to the spiky blond curls, I added some rouge to my caramel-colored cheeks and put a little MAC lip gloss on. Popping my lips, I smiled. With my perfectly white teeth lined up just right and my high cheekbones, along with my sexy body, I got out knowing I was the shit.

Inaya's ass needs to hurry and come help me with all these bags. I was already feeling the heat suck the life out of me as I reach down to unsnap and pick up a sleeping Q out of the teal Chico booster seat. Before I had a chance to turn all the way around, I could hear Naya screaming my name.

"Sahnaiiiiiii," she yelled while hugging me and dancing around. *Damn, baby cousin done lost some weight. I stayed away too long,* I thought sadly.

"Girl, I love ya, but hurry and show me which door is yours, because I'm about to drop this heavy-ass boy right over here in the grass and keep it moving. My back is not set up for heavy lifting." I got out as we both laughed and made our way to her front door.

After laying Q down in the guest bedroom that he and I would be sharing for a while, I went to grab our bags from the car. Dragging my Louie luggage, I swore I saw a familiar face as I walked through the parking lot. *Nah, it can't be him. Why would he even be up here?* Rochester was like the boonies to those Brooklyn boys, and I doubted he would have any reason to hang around this way.

I had to take a few seconds outside the door before I went in so Inaya's nosy ass didn't ask me any questions. The drive from DC wasn't that long, so I had no idea why I was tripping, imagining I saw Lox get into that Range Rover. All I saw of the guy was a glimpse of his face and then his back and his dreads anyway. I needed a drink ASAP. I knew it wasn't him, but there was just something about the way the guy walked.

Opening the door to my temporary home, I put it right out of my head.

"Naya, what's been up? You looking kinda stressed out. Once Qualyl wakes up, let's go get our feet and nails done, and when we come back I will fix up your hair."

"Cuz, honestly I don't have money to be doing none of that right now. I have to save every penny to meet the bills. I will let you do something to this head though. My hair was starting to fall out a few months ago," she calmly stated.

"I got you. Think of it as payment for letting us stay here and eat up your food and use up your toilet paper," I replied. Lucky for her she left it alone. I wasn't taking no for an answer.

As soon as Q got up, I was dropping him off to Grams's for the rest of the day with Miss Kadia. Grams swore she be missing the kids like crazy, and every time I would come for a visit she used to make me feel guilty about keeping her only great-grandson so far away.

"Sahnai, you think you gonna miss DC?"

"Naw, not really. It was a'ight. I mean, the malls and museums and shit was nice, but parking was a bitch. It was like the city all over again. I would get tons of parking tickets, and there was just too much traffic and people everywhere. Plus, I missed yo' little ass. Now enough about all of that. Come on and let's get ready to go," I told her as I went upstairs to change.

Chapter 11

Inaya

I knew I told my cousin no to the manicure and pedicure, but I was happy she said yes. I did have some money in my pockets, but it wouldn't be there long because that disrespectful-ass nigga Phantom struck again. After he came and gave me the best sex of my life and held me all night, I woke up to a stack of money and a cold bed. So I guessed he thought he could just fuck me and throw me some bands like I was a whore. Honestly he was only the third guy I had ever had sex with. I was only 21. I bet he didn't even know my age or shit else about me.

The more I thought about how careless he treated me, the angrier I got. I got angry at myself too. Why did I let him fuck or even come in my house? There was always some bullshit with him. I was convinced he was the devil with those black eyes and his magic dick. Gathering up the cash and shoving it in my Guess bag, I threw on some flip-flops and called out to Sahnai.

"Cuz, I will be right back. I am about to run next door because this nigga got me fucked up." Before she could respond, I was out my door and banging on his.

It was flung open, and I was once again staring into a frowned-up face, except this time I didn't care. Pushing past him into his front hall, I decided to make this quick. Shoving the money at him, I waited for him to take the hint and grab it.

"Look, I am not a whore or a thot you have to leave money on the bedside table for after you fuck me. I slept with you because I am feeling you, and I was in my feelings last night. I needed to be close to you, but I am going to tell you what I told you yesterday. Stay away from me."

His frown turned into a smirk, and I felt my hand automatically raise to slap the shit out of him. He caught my hand before I could make that mistake.

"Chill the fuck out, stupid. I left you the money not because we fucked, ma, but so you could be straight. You are Kades's mom, and I want her to be straight. So, Iny, keep the money, and get the fuck outta my face wit' all that noise."

Then he mushed my ass and shoved me out the door. Before I could even respond, I was looking at the cream paint on the front door.

"Urghhh!" *This nigga makes me so fucking mad.* Stomping into my house, I slammed the door before I remembered that I had company. Sahnai walked downstairs to see me holding a handful of cash with a mad look on my face.

"Well, bish, looks like you got your own money, so let's hit these streets," Sahnai said with a big-ass grin on her face. *I know she is just waiting on me to tell her more about Phantom, but I don't even know what to say. He is sexy but an asshole. I fucked him and don't even know his last name.*

Checking the mirror one more time, we popped our lips, walked to the car, and made our way to Orchid Nails. I was beginning to feel like the old me. I felt like the me before meeting Noah and having the weight of the world on my shoulders—happy, young, and carefree. I picked out my Tiffany blue nail polish and the silver sparkle overlay for my accent nail and big toe. Once that was laid over the blue it would look like I had diamonds all over that nail. Allowing the chair massage to relax me, I laid my head back and closed my eyes.

"So when I'ma meet this mysterious Phantom?"

As soon as the words left her mouth, I could feel my face turning bright red.

"Girl, ehhh. He is so fucking sexy, about five foot eleven, cocoa brown skin, and these eyes. When I look at his eyes, it's like I can barely think. They are black like the night sky and have a little chinky look to them. When he gets mad, though, his eyes get darker and his eyes and nose get all scrunched up. Girl, his body is, whoa, just perfect. He is cut in all the right places," I replied, fanning myself for effect.

"Wait, bish, how you know what his body looks like and what is right in what place? Let me find out you out here getting some from the guy next door," laughed Sahnai.

Ignoring my cousin's statement, I continued, "Phantom loves Kadia for whatever reason. When she went to the hospital the other day, he bought out damn near half the Toys 'R' Us. Girl, there was skates, Play-Doh, even a damn dollhouse with all the accessories. It took me an hour to carry all this shit to the house from the parking lot. I had to make like five trips."

"Wow, does Kadia like him? I know she is standoffish when it comes to men since everything with Noah."

"Here is the worst part: Kadia loves him. She is not even scared of him, and trust me, I was when I first met him. He looks like a damn menace. He even has a huge dragon tattoo down his arm and hand. None of that stops Kadia when she sees him. Shoot, it's like I don't even exist anymore. She throws up her little arms and puts on her best baby smile, and he picks her up and gives her whatever she wants."

"Well, damn, cuz. Maybe you need to start giving him the same smile and putting your hands up so he can swoop down and cuddle you and give you the wood . . . I mean, world."

By now Sahnai was laughing so hard the Asian nail tech was giving her one of those "hold the fuck still before I fuck up your toes" kind of looks.

"Honestly though, Sah, he is so mean to me. Sometimes he is nice, but mostly he is mean, and it is confusing as hell. He cussed me out about Kadia having an asthma attack, then about something else that had nothing to do with him. He has called me stupid and a thot, and worse, he doesn't even care who is watching."

"He sounds like a mess. Reminds me of someone I once knew in Brooklyn. He was the rudest nigga I ever knew."

As soon as our nails and toes were done and my almost-unibrow was gone, we went to the mall. Since I had some extra money, I didn't feel bad spending it this time. I allowed myself to buy a few outfits from Macy's and some sweatsuits from Victoria's Secret. Even though I bought Kadia some stuff the other day, I hit Children's Place and bought her some more summer clothes. School would be out in less than two weeks, and she would need some clothes to wear that were not school uniforms.

I followed Sahnai into this boutique called Exquisite.

"Get something for the club, Miss Thing, because we are going out tonight. I heard that it's going down at Temptations, or we can go to Euphoria. I can't believe that place is still around."

"What about this?" I asked, holding up a one-piece short romper in a coral color that had a gold chain around the waist. It had long sleeves and a deep V cut at the breast area.

"Yassss, girl! I love it!" shouted Sahnai after I tried it on. I had to admit I liked it too, because it made my little butt and my boobs pop out. Twirling around the dressing room and looking in the mirror, I felt pretty for the first time in a while.

"Come on, sis, let me buy it for you."

I ended up with tie-up gold sandals, too, and some gold accessories.

"Look, Naya, I can tell something has been up with you lately, but I am here for you no matter what. I am happy you found someone who makes you smile, even though you say he ain't feeling you. I can tell something is there. Now let's go turn up."

Chapter 12

Lox

I hope this nigga Phantom is home. I left my key in the house when I ran out, and I did not feel like waiting for his ass. He liked to roam the streets until nine or ten the next morning. He had so many cars I could never tell when this nigga was here, and he was not answering his phone. *Fuck it, I'm going to knock on the door.* Walking up the path, I saw Inaya, Kadia, and another female behind her walking to the school bus.

"Hey, Inaya, what's up, ma? You seen Phantom?"

Ha-ha, yeah, she was feeling my cousin, because when I mentioned his name, her face was twisted into the meanest-ass look, but her eyes lit up, and her skin turned red.

"I don't see Phantom, and not much is up. Getting ready to go to work after this one gets off to school," she said, waving her hand in Kadia's direction. I was happy to see she looked much better than when I saw her in the mall last week. She had her hair looking shiny and laid straight down her back, her eyebrows were arched, and her face was filling back out, not looking so sunken in. I could see the beauty in her even though she had on khaki work pants and an ugly-ass yellow T-shirt. She looked datable.

Phantom told me he left some money for her and Kades after I told him how she couldn't buy the baby sneakers. I was glad to see baby girl was wearing the new white-on-white Uptowns I bought her the other day. It looked like they matched her little plaid school uniform best. "Hey, Kades. How is your morning, little one?" I made a point to speak to her. Phantom brought her to the park and shit when we played soccer, and sometimes she came to the house, so I had gotten to know her a little bit. She was smart for only being 4 years old, and she really brought out the sweet side in my cousin.

"Hey, Uncle Lox, I am good. I am so happy my baby cousin is here visiting so I can have someone to play with. He is so cute, just like a baby doll, and he has weird eyes like yours," she rambled on and on, but I stopped listening as soon as I got a good look at the girl standing with Inaya. As soon as I saw the tears falling from her eyes, I knew it was her. *How dare she be standing in front of me like she doesn't even know me? After everything we went through, she was going to just walk on by.* I could feel myself getting pissed the fuck off.

Grabbing her by her throat, I was only stopped by Kadia's cry and a sudden pain in my balls. Damn, I forgot Sahnai fought dirty. Her ass kneed me in the fucking balls.

"Wow, really, Sahnai? You was gonna walk by your nigga and not say a word? Oh, yeah, foolish fucking me. I just thought I was yo' nigga, but I guess it was someone else. I gave you the whole fucking world, but it wasn't enough, right?" I got out while bending over in pain.

"Lennox, stop it. You don't understand. I had to leave. I love you, and I have never stopped loving you, but I had to protect myself. I couldn't stay, and no, I can't tell you why. I'm sorry for hurting you and walking out on you, but I did what was best for everybody," she got out in between trying to catch her breath and sobbing.

Everything in me wanted to hold her until she calmed down and kiss her pretty face, but the "I don't give a fuck" part of me wanted to keep choking her out and not listen to the pleas she was throwing my way.

"Sahnai, you were the one. I know I never told you, but I showed you every way I could that I loved you. Yeah, I cheated sometimes, but I never let a girl come to you and disrespect you. I never let anything tear you down."

"Umm, well, I was going to introduce you to my cousin Sahnai, but it looks like you already know her. I am taking Kadia to the bus stop now, and, Lox, if you put your hands on my cousin again, I will cut you the fuck up," Inaya threatened as Phantom walked up the path and grabbed her arm, dragging her away. The whole time I could hear him telling Kades that Sahnai and I were playing a game and that I would never hurt her auntie because we were old friends. Then he promised her doughnuts and a ride to school in any car she wanted. Her giggles let me know she was cool, but I felt bad for scaring her. I guessed I was going to be hitting Toys "R" Us later on, too.

Now that it was just Sahnai and me standing there, I didn't even know what to say to her. Was there even anything left to say? *Wait, Kadia said she was playing with her baby cousin.* Did Sahnai have a baby?

"Sahnai, you got a baby, yo? And don't fucking lie," I said with the meanest face I could produce.

Her eyes got real big, and her face turned white as a sheet of paper as she ran back toward the house. Nothing else needed to be said. Her face said it all. My chest hurt. It felt like that time I fell off the top of the gully when I was a kid and all the air was sucked out of my body. This shit hurt. I thought she left me because she wasn't ready to settle down, but instead she went and had a kid with another nigga. This was worse than her kicking me in the balls.

"Sahnai, this shit ain't over. We not done talking, so don't go far. Oh, yeah, and tell your bitch-ass baby daddy he better not bring his ass this way or he gonna see me," I barked after her. Now my whole vibe was fucked up. Looking in my phone, I decided to get some stress released. I called this little bad bitch I met last time I went out. Candy was her name. Yeah, I know that name makes you think, *stripper,* but she was actually a bartender.

"Yo, Candy, what's up, ma? You hungry?"

"Nothing, Lox. I'm at home cleaning up. Yeah, I could eat. Meet me at Applebee's by the mall."

"Cool."

Speeding the whole way there, I was just happy I didn't get a ticket or wreck my whip. The first thing I did once seated was order a drink while I waited for Candy. I couldn't believe I just saw Sahnai. I spent so many days and nights wondering why she left me and where she went. I wouldn't hustle or nothing when she first disappeared. I killed a few of my enemies just in case they had anything to do with it. Phantom had to take care of all our business. I just sat around drinking and smoking weed all day.

Candy walked in a few minutes later, not really giving me time to figure out what I was going to do about Sahnai. I guessed I should have skipped trying to eat and just met shawty at the crib so I could bust a nut. I needed that shit bad right now. Candy was a cute chick. She had a little shape to her body and dressed nicely. Today she had on a colorful sundress and strappy white sandals. Her plum and black hair was cut into a nice bob, and her makeup was on point. The lipstick even matched the color of her hair. She had a tiny face with close-set eyes and a little button nose.

Once we'd ordered our food, I just sat back and let her talk. Females love to chitchat. She was talking about how she didn't get enough tips at work and people were mean and they should respect her job. It all sounded like blah, blah, blah after a while. I couldn't get my mind to focus on anything she was saying. By the time we had finished eating I was bored out of my mind, and I wanted to go see what the hell Sahnai was doing or fall asleep.

"Ma, I'ma follow you to your crib, a'ight?"

"A'ight, boo, let's go," she said while licking her lips, trying to make a sexy face.

Once we got to the spot, I jumped out and followed her into the living room. Candy's crib was all right, nothing to scream about, but it wasn't dirty or anything like that. I sat on the leather couch and pulled my man out while she went to get me a bottle of water.

"Damn, just like that, huh?" she said while smiling and dropping to her knees.

Yeah, just what I needed, or so I thought. My nigga was dead in the water. Maybe she didn't notice because my shit was big and thick to begin with, and I was sure it was over ten inches when fully ready. But I wouldn't know exactly because I wasn't a bitch nigga who watched Porn Hub to get it up or measured it with a ruler or nothing.

No matter how much she slurped, spat, tugged, and licked, my man was bored. I had never had this problem before. I felt like I was cheating on Sahnai now that I'd seen her, but that was crazy. We were not together. *She moved on and left me, so fuck her. Well, I guess it's fuck me, because I can't even bust this nut I want to.*

"A'ight, ma, get up. I'm good on that. I have to make a run. Some niggas on the team been giving me a lot of trouble, so I got a lot on my mind. I'ma go handle that and holla at you when I got my mind right," I explained as I got up and made my way to the door, not even looking back.

Chapter 13

Inaya

"Yo, I'ma just drop you off at work and pick you back up, so we can take Kadia to school," demanded Phantom as he opened the doors to the Bentley so we could climb in. *I guess I don't have a fucking choice,* I wanted to say, but the way my raggedy-ass car be acting, I was relieved to have a ride, especially one with AC.

"Just take a right at Winton, and her school is on Elmwood on your side." Before I knew it, we were pulling up to Our Lady of Mercy Catholic School, and Kadia was waving goodbye, leaving Phantom and me alone. I never thought that was a good idea, but whatever.

After a few minutes I wondered why we were just sitting there. She was long gone in the school, and I was about to be late for work.

"Yo, Iny, you gonna tell me where you work at?"

I had to laugh out loud because I was clearly in my own world. "Sorry, on Clinton and Clifford at Childtime Day Care."

When we pulled up, he came around and opened my door, and before I could stop him, he pulled my body close and leaned up against the car.

"What time you get off?" he asked quietly.

"Four o'clock," I replied, pulling away from him and making my way inside.

As soon as I clocked in, took my shoes off, and put on my slippers, I went into the baby room to start my day. Turning on all the lights, I began putting out the Boppies and opening the blinds. I loved working with the babies, and I wished I were the lead teacher in here. They made more money and were guaranteed hours. They even gave them benefits.

Speak of the devil, in walked the lead teacher, Teresa, and my other coworker, Jala. She was her sidekick, aka Miss Kiss Ass. I felt like I did a great job with the babies. They loved me, and kissing Teresa's ass was not in my job description. Especially not no hood rat bitch's who would be making $8 an hour for the rest of her life.

"Morning," they both chimed at the same time with big ol' smiles on their faces. Oh, I could tell these nosy hoes were watching me in the parking lot when Phantom dropped me off.

"Morning," I dryly responded while continuing to get the room ready.

"So how do you know Phantom?" Jala began the conversation that I was not interested in having.

"He is a friend of mine. Why?"

"Girl, he is the man in the streets. You better hold on to that friend, because he is fine, and he got long pockets."

"Thanks, Jala, but we are not that kind of friendly. More like acquaintances. He was nice enough to give me a ride since my car has been acting up, and Kadia missed her bus because of his cousin."

"Girl, if you don't want him, I will take his ass. I will poke holes in every condom in the box and be any kind a freak he wants me to be in the bed. Once I get that baby, I am quitting this job and spending all that nigga money. You need to get me his number," Teresa said while giving Jala a high five and laughing.

Rolling my eyes, I went to greet my first parent of the day and switched my mind to the drama with Sahnai this morning. I noticed she never mentioned Q to Lox. Anyone with eyes could see he was his son, and he did not seem like he knew they had a kid together, so when he found out, she would really be in for it. Not many people had those long eyelashes and green cat eyes, so she could save any lies she was thinking of. *I can't believe she told all the family Q's father was killed and that is why she moved to DC.*

I was not sure why she would leave and take Lox's baby away. He seemed nice, and he was sexy. He definitely had more manners than his rude-ass cousin. I couldn't wait to go home, because I wanted all the details. *This nigga better not be late picking me up. Shoot, I don't even have his number in case he is running behind so I can call and remind him of the time.*

Normally work dragged, especially toward the end of the day when I was stuck with the same two babies every day waiting to go home because their parents were always late. At 3:45, I noticed Phantom while looking out the window. He pulled up and leaned against his truck while talking on his cell phone. He was so sexy to me. I wished I could get him out of my system because, like a drug, he was no good for me. I could feel myself getting jealous because whoever he was talking to on the other end had him laughing and smiling. He had a nice smile, and I would give anything for him to smile at me like that.

After I finished off the highchairs and sanitizing the toys, I turned to shut the blinds just in time to see Jala slipping a piece of paper in Phantom's hand and giving him what she thought was a sexy walk as she headed to the bus stop. Sadly, he put it right in his pocket and kept talking on his phone to another one of his women. Oh, yeah, I knew it was a bitch, because no man smiled like that into the phone while talking to another man.

Going outside, I made a silent promise to not engage in any conversation with him on the way home. *Just look out the window and mind my own business until I get where I am going.*

When I climbed in the passenger side, he told whomever he was on the phone with he loved her and would see her and the boys soon. Even though I didn't want to care, my feelings were hurt. *He must want nothing with me since he was talking to his woman and kids' mother right in front of me.*

"How was work, Iny? You're quiet today. Everything all right?"

"Work was fine," I responded. "Phantom, let me ask you something. Do you have kids?"

The biggest laugh I ever heard from him came out of his mouth.

"First off, ma, just ask if I was talking to my woman right beside you. Second of all, I won't lie and disrespect my daughter's memory even though it hurts to mention her. I have one daughter who passed away. She would have been three in July, and her name was Cassandra. I don't have any other kids. I have three bad-ass nephews. I was talking to their mother, who is my little sister Azia. Anything else you would like to know?"

Feeling bold since he was talking, I decided to go for a few more questions.

"Well, since you asked, how old are you? When is your birthday, and what is your favorite color?"

"I am twenty-six, my birthday was April second, and my favorite color is black."

I made fun of him about black not really being a color, and he asked me some questions, and it went on this way the whole ride home. By the time we were pulling up to the parking lot and he was dropping me off, I felt like I knew Phantom for the first time. He wasn't just a neighbor or a man I fucked the other night. He was my friend.

Chapter 14

Lox

I had been out of town the past few days following the person who made a pickup for us from Florida. The last time this same cat came up short, so I was following to see if he had any funny business going on. I asked my cousin to get Sahnai's number from Iny for me, and sure enough, she gave it up. I had been texting and calling her the whole time I was on the road and even got her to FaceTime me once. It was just like old times except she now had a kid, and I didn't know what she'd been doing the past few years.

She did tell me she lived in DC and had to leave Brooklyn because someone was going to hurt her. I wished she had just come to me. I could have protected her. I felt like shit when I thought about the fact that she didn't feel safe with me. She didn't trust that I could have taken care of anyone who was a threat to her. It made me want to find the person and shoot them in the face for making the love of my life run away from me. One thing she did say, that she wasn't even my girl back then, was true. I lost out when I didn't make it official. It wasn't because I didn't know I wanted her. It was because I didn't want to stop fucking other girls, even though I still tried to hide any other bitches from her.

I asked her if she missed DC, and she told me hell no. It was hectic there, and the prices of rent, car insurance, and everything else were way overpriced, especially in the city. She also said it was no place to raise kids. I could understand wanting to raise ya shorty somewhere quiet.

I asked about her son, and she told me how old he was and that he was her light through all the dark times. I could hear the love in her voice as she talked about him, and it made me think she must have really loved his father. I guessed she had him after she and I broke up right the fuck after. A little part of me was hoping she would say he was mine, but then I would have wanted to kill her for keeping my kid from me. She did tell me his pops was dead, so even though I was sad for li'l man, I was happy I had no competition in the way. *I ain't have no problem stepping in and being a father to him.*

"Sahnai, what you up to, ma?" I called and asked her once I got in the house. Even though I was tired I wanted to see her face.

"Me and Inaya are looking at a few places for me to move into. I think I found the one I love in Henrietta. It has two walk-in closets with his-and-her sinks in the bathroom. I even have a playroom like Iny has at her place and a pool for the kids. Kadia will be trying to move in." Even though I laughed I was sad she wouldn't be in the same spot as me anymore, even though she would only be about five minutes away.

"A'ight, ma, come meet me at the house, and I will hit you wit' some bread for the rent and security and shit," I told her.

"Nah, Lox, I'm cool. It's taken care of. I will stop and say hey once I get there though."

I guess I have to be happy wit' that.

"A'ight, hurry up. I wanna see you." I hurried and jumped in the shower and threw on some Nike basketball shorts and a white wife-beater. An hour later she was knocking on the door. Trying to balance two drinks in one hand and a bag of food in the other, she stood outside with an impatient look on her face. I opened the door to let her in and took the food from her before she dropped my dinner.

"Sorry it took so long. I had to settle my son in, and I got us some food."

Opening the bag, I could see she still remembered my favorite foods. She got me shrimp fried rice and a seafood special with a side of sesame chicken. I also saw she was eating the same ol' thing: sesame chicken and white rice with a side of broccoli.

"Sahnai, you know, you can bring li'l man over here wit' you. Kadia be coming over here all the time. We don't bite little kids or nothing. Now that I think about it, I never even seen your baby. You sure you got a kid, yo?"

She had an uncomfortable look on her face. "He is not good with strangers, so it is easier to leave him with Inaya. Thank you for inviting him over though."

I turned on the sixty-inch TV in the living room and moved the food in there. I hit Netflix and handed her the remote. She used to love to control the TV and watch what she wanted all the time. Honestly, I was a flexible kind of nigga when it came to that. I would watch anything except that fucking old lady show she liked, *The Golden Girls*. Those old broads used to creep me out, especially the one who thought she was sexy.

"Let's watch this," she said, clicking on some series called *The Blacklist*. Even though I'd just driven twenty hours, she couldn't hang and was slumped after one episode. I decided to keep her with me tonight. Carrying her upstairs, I slid off her gray leggings and left her in her white T-shirt and silk blue panties. Climbing in beside her and wrapping my arms around her, I held her until I fell asleep.

***

"Morning, babes." I smiled as soon as I woke up to see her walking in the room.

"Lox, I am going to run next door and get some eggs or something so I can make breakfast, because you ain't got shit up in here," she said as she slid on her leggings and prepared to go downstairs.

"Nah, it's cool. Let's go to breakfast at IHOP. I remember how much you love they pancakes. You want to go get baby boy and bring him with us?"

"Yeah, we should go get breakfast, and naw, he is good where he at," she said, walking into my bathroom and helping herself to an extra toothbrush. I mean, damn, was her kid disabled or something? She kept ignoring me when I asked about him. I tried to sneak and see if she had a picture of him in her phone last night, but the phone was locked.

When she walked out of the bathroom, her face was glowing. You would have thought I gave her the D or something the way her face was all lit up. When she started making the bed and picking up my dirty clothes, it felt just like the old days.

"Come on, let's go eat. A nigga belly 'bout to cave in, ma," I said, grabbing her hand and rushing her out the door. I was one of those dudes with a big-ass appetite, and I was not ashamed of it either.

I couldn't help but grab Sahnai's ass as she climbed into the Range Rover.

"Boy, leave me alone," she cried out, but I could hear the smile in her voice.

By the time we pulled in to IHOP, I thought I was going to fall out from hunger. *I hope these motherfuckers are quick with their service.* Usually I drank a protein shake in the morning, but I remembered Sahnai hates those, so I decided to make it about her.

Sliding into the booth across from her, I smiled as I watched her order exactly what I knew she would: one waffle with ice cream on top, a steak medium well, and sunny-side up eggs with cheese.

I ordered a stack of blueberry pancakes, a bowl of fruit, and scrambled eggs. We both got our favorite fresh strawberry lemonades.

"Sahnai, promise you won't run away again, ma. I don't care who it is threatening you on the real. No nigga out here put fear in my heart, and I will always be that nigga for you."

"Honestly, Lox, I can't promise you that I won't ever leave again, but I will promise to not leave without telling you. I know you want to reassure me about the threat I have, but this is not something you could understand, and the threat is still around. The bottom line is I have my son to keep safe, and he has to remain the most important person in my life."

I had to accept that answer from her because it was better than nothing. I really wanted to ask her why she wouldn't let me help her with her new place and how she could afford to do it on her own, but I left it alone. I mean, we'd been out of each other's lives for over two years now, and I couldn't just come in here running shit, at least not right away.

As soon as the waitress slid us the check and we stood up to go and pay, I knew shit was about to go from pleasant to not so pleasant just that quickly. Candy was walking toward me with one of those "I am on my period, and I want to scratch your eyes out" kind of faces.

Grabbing Sahnai's hand and walking to the front, I was hoping Candy would get the hint and keep it moving, but no such luck.

"Hey, Lox, I guess this whore is why you couldn't come back and finish the sex session we started the other day, right?" she asked in an angry voice.

Before I could respond, Sahnai opened her mouth and gave her what she was looking for. "Nice to meet you, Miss Pop Off. Yeah, I am his whore, bitch, rider, wifey, whatever you want to call me. I am all of that and his personal stripper, too. So what you should do is crawl out of your feelings and go buy yourself breakfast like you was doing in the first place." With that she opened the door, and out we went. I could hear Candy cursing me out and all the other people in the restaurant laughing at her as the door clicked behind us.

"Sahnai, you wild. I'm taking your ass home before you beat up every girl I fuck wit'."

The whole ride back to the house she was rapping along to Dej Loaf's "Try Me" and bopping around in her seat all hyped up. I guessed she was playing that song for Candy. *Ha-ha.*

As soon as I pulled up, I kissed her and made sure I had my tongue down her throat. She hopped out with a smile and a wave.

"Later," she called.

We all had a meeting at the main spot, so I rode across town to be on time since I knew Phantom's ass was always late. If this nigga had to work a nine-to-five, he would have killed the boss, offended every customer and worker, or been fired for never making it on time.

Pulling up to the brick house at the end of the one-way street, I saw Phine and JRock sitting on the front steps drinking Guinness.

"What's up, Lox?" they greeted me.

"Shit, I can't call it. Just trying to survive," I replied.

"Yo, Lox, you fucking that bitch Sahnai? I seen you and her today over on Jefferson."

I could feel the veins in my neck tightening and my heartbeat start to speed up as soon as he mentioned Sahnai's name. "Why?" I asked.

"Yo, boss, I'm just trying to warn you that bitch is a gold digger. I just gave her ten stacks to move, and she ain't even let a nigga hit yet. I hope she know as soon as she move into her new place, I am digging in her guts. Shorty is fine as fuck though. I heard she take any nigga money she come across, so just stay safe and protect your pockets." Phine finished this with a laugh.

Getting up, I walked to my truck as Phantom was pulling up.

"Yo, cuz, what's wrong wit' you?" he asked, but I kept walking. Reaching in the back seat, I grabbed ten stacks and walked back to the house.

"Yo, my man, hold this, and don't ever contact Sahnai again, you hear me? She ain't no gold digger. You a fucking trick, and she don't need shit else from you. I promise I better not hear you ever say her name again. Delete her phone number, and go find a new girl to try to freak," I told his punk ass as I threw the money in his face and walked away.

"Lox, yo, man, what the fuck is going on?" Phantom was calling me, but I hopped in my ride and peeled off.

After driving around for a few hours, I was mad at Sahnai. *Why the fuck is she out here taking these niggas' money when she know I got this? She just took ten stacks from a li'l nigga who works for me. I want to go and slap her in the fucking face. I mean, she is making herself look like a fucking thot, and she has not a care in the world. Plus, she is embarrassing me. I mean, what do I look like with the queen by my side being the bitch every nigga in town is talking about?*

Taking out my phone, I called Tee, this little cute bitch I fucked with sometimes.

"Yo, Tee, let a nigga see you today, ma," I kind of told her instead of asking her. I knew she wasn't turning me down. I met her at one of my soccer practices. She and her ratchet friends used to come a lot and watch us practice. I was used to that shit, these chicks showing up every day and hanging out watching us, hoping to catch a baller or some dick. I guessed she caught the dick.

"Well, I am on my way to work, so probably not today," she replied.

I know this bitch think she is slick, but I got this one.

"Yo, ma, just call in, and I will give you two hundred dollars for the day. Meet me at the Holiday Inn by the airport, and hit me when you get there."

I bet I just made her day. Shit, I bet she didn't even have to work today but just wanted to get me for some cash. I knew she didn't make more than $70 a day at whatever bullshit job she was working. I could have saved the hotel money and met her at her place, but I went there once, and it looked like a Garbage Pail Kid's house. I couldn't believe she was a mom. It was absolutely gross in there.

Pulling up to the hotel, I got a basic room with a full-size bed and texted her the room number. Once Tee got there, she came in and took off her raincoat. She had nothing on under, and I guessed she thought that shit was sexy. Maybe on someone else. I mean, she was cute, but a girl with a dirty house and little ambition was only that. *She does suck a mean dick though.*

She started on her knees, and I wasted no time grabbing her by her fake hair and gagging her. I could feel my legs shake as she took all of me in the back of her throat and sucked me dry. She once told me she gave such good head because she had her tonsils removed. I didn't know if that shit was true, but I wasn't complaining.

She lay on the bed rubbing her freshly shaved pussy and gapping her legs open.

"Baby, taste it for me one time," she said in her sexy voice. I pretended I didn't hear as I slid my Magnum on and turned her over. I roughly entered her from be-hind and fucked her hard and fast.

"Lox, stop. It hurts," she screamed out. I couldn't stop if I wanted to. I grabbed her by her neck and started choking her to shut her the fuck up until I could get my nut off. I could feel her running, so I choked her a little harder until I could feel my dick hit bottom.

"Yes, bitch. Don't fucking move," I yelled as I filled the condom and collapsed on top of her.

Check Out Receipt

Harold Washington Library Center

Thursday, March 2, 2023 3:16:17 PM

Item: R0464915821
Title: Hometown reunion
Due: 3/23/2023

Item: R0464887701
Title: The bronc rider's twins
Due: 3/23/2023

Item: R0464904511
Title: Protecting Colton's baby
Due: 3/23/2023

Item: R0458151689
Title: Fourplay : the dance of
sensuality
Due: 3/23/2023

Item: R0464406822
Title: Taking down a boss
Due: 3/23/2023

Item: R0462099679
Title: My heart beats for you
Due: 3/23/2023

Total items: 6

Thank you.

1238

Chapter 15

Inaya

Looking at my phone, I saw alerts showing me I had a few texts from Phantom. He was asking me and Kadia to come to the soccer match out in Churchville today. I decided it may be a good idea to get out of the house while I was looking cute. I had just put on a pair of short white shorts and a lime green strappy shirt from Bebe. The front was slanted so you could see my belly ring that had stars hanging from the stud, and the back was open a bit, showing my tattoo of Kadia's name in a heart. I finally got Sahnai to give me some illusion braids so I could get up and go and not iron or curl my hair on a daily basis. I was beginning to feel like I worked in a hair shop as much as I was handling those tools. She used honey blond and a little bit of blond and red hair to braid into my own, and it looked adorable.

I let Phantom know we were on our way, and then I went to go and get Kadia ready and see if Sahnai would go with me.

"Sahnai, you want to go watch the guys play soccer at the park out in Churchville? They have a game at one."

"Girl, I want to, but I can't bring Q and chance Lox or anyone else seeing him. I don't want to die today," she laughed, but I knew she was serious, because I thought Lox was going to kill her when he eventually found out about Q being his baby.

Even though I understood why she did what she did back then and ran away and never told him about his son, she had to understand that that was then and this was now, the baby was already here, and I didn't think he would feel the same way as he did back then. Maybe he was just young and scared, or young and dumb. I almost wondered if she misunderstood, because he didn't seem like the type to behave that way, but what did I know? Shit, I did know I didn't want to go alone, so we had to figure this out.

"Just call Grams, and ask if we can take Nadia with us, and she can keep the kids at the park."

After she thought about it for a minute, she responded, "Yeah, that's a great idea. The park is kinda far from the field, and we don't have to stay until the end anyway. Let me go get ready and we can leave. I know Nadia will be happy to get out of the house anyway."

Nadia was our cousin Rich's daughter. She was 13 and lived with our grandmother because her mom and dad were in jail. She was a good kid and helped a lot with the little ones.

Once Kadia found out we were going to the soccer game, she put on her little pink and white soccer jersey and white shorts with some white and pink Nike cleats. I had no idea where they came from or where the whole outfit came from. She was looking cute with her hair braided up in a zigzag design with clear and white beads on the ends and matching knockers in the ponytail. With every step she took, her hair would make a clicking noise, and she would laugh. As we walked out the door, she even produced a purple soccer ball made for kids. I just shook my head. *Phantom is turning her into a little boy or a mini Phantom.*

I was starting to get worried about the amount of time she spent with him. He and I still didn't have a title, and

I noticed her calling him Daddy sometimes, too, instead of Phantom. I had to put a stop to that. I didn't want her to get hurt or confused, and I didn't want him to feel pressured. I was going to bring it up to him later on so I could start correcting her and let her know she needed to call him Phantom.

As soon as we all piled into Sahnai's BMW and stopped to pick up Nadia, we were on our way. I was excited that Phantom invited me to watch him in the game. I felt like we were getting somewhere. We texted and talked every day, and he even let me borrow his black Audi last week because the alternator on my car went out, and that was not in my budget at the moment.

As we pulled into the parking lot, Q was fast asleep, which always happened in the car. That was his nap spot.

"Just grab his stroller, pull the shade down, and put a blanket over the top. It will be fine," I said to ease Sahnai's nerves.

She looked like she was going to grab the baby and run away with him like a mother bear and her baby cub. Her stroller looked like a damn rocket ship. She always did like fancy, expensive shit. Once she put it together and laid Q in it, she threw his light blue blanket over the top so only his little Jordans stuck out below.

I did understand how stressful this situation could be, and I also knew that was why she found a place to move fast, even though I wished she had stayed with me longer. Shit, I be lonely, and when she was there it was like a sleepover or girls' night every night.

After we sat on the bench watching the guys (Phantom was rude in soccer too), they took a halftime break. As Phantom jogged over to us, no one could even speak to him because Kadia ran and jumped in his arms and began running down the whole game, her morning, and anything else she could talk about. Looking at me, he winked, and we shared a smile.

"So that's why you didn't give a fuck if our baby lived or died. You already had a little girl. See, this is why Cassandra had to go, because I needed your attention, and all along you were giving it to another family," said a lady who was shockingly pretty, had a perfect shape, and had curves in all the right places. She had flawless skin with cheekbones like a model and long jet-black hair in wavy, loose curls. The only flaw was that her eyes looked crazy.

"Yo, Shawnie, go on from here. You killed Cassandra, not me. If you don't move from here, I am going to remember how I want you to die and just shoot you between the eyes," Phantom threatened while handing Kadia to Lox and walking closer to the girl.

As if she just realized I was there, she locked eyes on me and felt I was a threat to her fantasy of her and Phantom having a happily ever after.

"Oh, so you're the baby's mother. Bitch, I am going to fuck you up. You are also responsible for me losing my man because his daughter died. You are nothing to him. I will always be his first love," she shouted as she grabbed my hair and pulled me off the bench. I wasn't expecting that, so she got a one up on me, but my survival mode kicked in, and I kicked her in the leg. Once she fell on the ground, I picked up a brick and smashed her body and face with it until she was choking on that.

"Bitch, I am wifey now but never knew him in your time. So stay the fuck away from my man, and we won't have any problems. And I gotcho bitch. Say it one more time."

Walking to Phantom, I could see the looks on everybody's faces. Yeah, I was quiet, but I grew up in the hood, and if you came for me, I would come for you.

"Let's go," I said, grabbing Phantom's hand in one of mine and Kadia's in the other. We left even though it was still halftime. Nadia and Sahnai beat me to the car, and somehow Q was in the car seat and his baby shade was down in minutes.

"Sahnai, I will bring her and Kades home. You are free to go without her," Phantom informed her.

"All right, and, cuz, you a beast wit' dem hands. I love you, and I will see you later," Sahnai said as she climbed in her car and pulled out of the lot, leaving a trail of dust behind.

Chapter 16

Phantom

I was still shocked as hell that little crybaby Inaya handled Shawnie like that. I was proud of her though. Plus, I was glad she had a backbone, because if she was going to fuck with a nigga like me, a lot of girls were going to test her—niggas, too—and in my line of business, I may have had to make a move anytime and not be there to protect her and Kades. She would have to learn how to protect herself. *Maybe I should take her to the gun range and get her some lessons.*

"Phantom, you not mad, are you?" she asked me in her little, low voice.

"Mad? Naw, ma, I ain't mad at all. I got my own little Mike Tyson now. A nigga feel all safe and shit," I teased her, trying to get her to laugh. It worked and she laughed.

As soon as we turned in to the complex, I picked up Kadia, and we walked to the door. "Man, what you feeding her? She weigh like a thousand pounds. I am cutting her allowance."

"Boy, please, she ain't that heavy, and allowance for what? She is not old enough to do any chores without my help, so I earned that," she told me as we made it to my door.

"Iny, come stay with me tonight. You and Kades. She can sleep in her room."

"Sure. She can sleep in her what?"

"Well, we have two extra bedrooms here, and she kind of took over one. I even bought her a pretty comforter and a few toys. Nothing big," I lied.

Once we made it upstairs to lay her down, I could see the look on Iny's face. Okay, so Kadia's room in my house was a little bit awesome. Anyway, I honestly didn't give her the whole room. I made half for my nephews with bunk beds and a dinosaur theme. Kadia's side had pink, purple, and orange butterflies everywhere and a canopy bed with matching bedding. A flat screen was on the wall with an Xbox and Wii U, and her toy box overflowed with dolls and accessories.

"Okay, I guess it is a bit much, but when she saw the boys had a room, she wanted in on it, and I have a hard time telling her no."

"Clearly," she dryly replied.

"Iny, come lie wit' me. I want to talk to you about some stuff, okay?"

Following me to the bed, she slid off her clothes, slid on one of my T-shirts, and slid in next to me. I felt like I should tell Iny the truth about me and Shawnie and our situation. Trying to buy myself some time, I decided to go take a piss and brush my teeth. Talking about this part of my past was hard for me. Silently hoping she would be asleep when I got out, I was not in luck. I walked in and saw her sitting up in bed watching some strange yard sale show. I slipped in next to her, and she turned toward me and sat Indian style, tilting her head to the side the way she often did when she was waiting.

"Look, about Shawnie, first off, I am sorry she approached you like that. She had no right to act like that toward you, because I straight up don't fuck wit' her."

"Do you still love her? She was your baby moms, and a lot of men go back to their baby moms for a taste or two."

"Naw, Iny. I would never fuck her, and that is on my sister's life. I could be high, horny, and drunk, and I wouldn't look her way. Remember I told you I had a daughter named Cassandra who passed away?"

"Yeah." She nodded her head.

"Shawnie was Cassandra's mom. When I found out that she was pregnant, I was not looking to settle down or anything. Shawnie was just a casual female friend who I slipped and fucked raw once or twice. But since I did not want to be like my dad, I decided I would take a chance at this settling down thing. Now Shawnie was a fucking hot-head and turned every little thing into a huge argument. I was still young and knew I wasn't perfect, but a nigga was really trying. Anyway, I got us a crib in Brooklyn with two bedrooms, and I told Shawnie to quit her CNA job and stay home to prepare for the baby.

"Once Cassandra was born, I fell in love. She was so pretty and had perfect brown skin and my black eyes. She had silky jet-black hair and heart-shaped lips. I spent almost every free moment I had with her. I would take her with me a lot because Shawnie was so jealous of the baby. She wanted me to be all about her and not our daughter.

"Iny, I swear something was telling me not to leave my daughter with her, but I had to go on the road to handle something. This was after Sahnai left, and Lox was a wreck. If only I had taken her to Azia or my aunt, anybody else. But I didn't. I was in Florida making a pickup, and I had been calling and calling Shawnie for two days to check on my baby. I was sick to my stomach with worry and fear. I just knew something was up.

"When I got home and saw police cars and an ambulance in front of our building with the lights flashing, I knew that she did something to my baby. The rest is kind of a blur, but I remember running over to the ambulance and telling the police I was looking for my daughter. She was lying there on the stretcher with an oxygen mask covering her tiny face, and her fingers were blue.

"She killed my daughter, her own daughter. She laid her in the bathtub at seven months old and walked away while our baby drowned. If the police didn't already have her, I would have killed her with my bare hands. She went to jail for a year until they said she had postpartum depression and let her go. After seeing her today after all this time, I think she is actually crazy, not depressed. I still plan to kill her when the time is right. I want to torture her and then drown her like she did Cassandra."

It felt so good to tell someone what happened. I had never told anyone except my family, and even then I spared them a lot of the details. When I looked at Inaya, she was sobbing with her hand shoved in her mouth.

"Shhhh, it's okay. I pray a lot, especially for my baby. It hurts, but it taught me many hard lessons."

Chapter 17

Sahnai

I had been in my new place for a week, and it was finally feeling like home. I got the upgraded unit with a Jacuzzi tub and a new dishwasher thanks to my sponsor, Phine. He didn't even ask any questions when I told him I needed to get my own space and could use some money to make it happen, although he had been calling every day since I moved in, asking when he could come and see the place. I knew he thought he was getting some of this pussy, but that wasn't happening. I made niggas wait a long time, and we had to be in a relationship before I was fucking. I was far from a ho. I was just okay with dumb niggas spending their money on me. Shit, someone had to spend it.

On the real I liked Phine. He had dark skin and was six feet tall, and he had gold fronts on his bottom teeth and tiny ears you didn't really notice because his waves were on point, but they were cute anyway. I loved that he kept his nails manicured, and he made good conversation. We went bowling and to Dave & Buster's, and he was not a boring dude or anything like that. It was just that, since Lox came back into my life, I couldn't focus on any other man. I still loved him, but hiding Q from him complicated things. Could I still love a man who didn't want our baby? Or one who would hate me for keeping his son

from him? For now, what we had going on was working,
I guessed.

My ex-friend in DC kept calling me, asking to come
and chill. He'd still been putting money into my PayPal
account, so I had money coming in. Honestly, I didn't
need their money. I had almost $100,000 saved up. I just
liked to spend other people's money.

I was thinking about opening my own hair salon. I
wanted it to be unique and stay open twenty-four hours a
day for five days a week and by appointment on the other
two days. I wanted to put in a nail bar and a massage
center and serve wine to my customers while they waited.

I was so caught up in my daydream about my future,
I forgot that Lox was coming over today. I was kind
of excited to have him come and see the place I had. I
worked hard to get into this place, and it was gorgeous.
It had granite countertops, an island, plush carpeting,
the works. I decided to cook him some dinner since I
knew his ass was greedy. Taking out the frying pan and a
pot, I boiled some cauliflower and fried us some chicken
breasts. I cooked jasmine rice and made homemade
carrot juice. I figured that should make him happy.

As soon as I set the table, he was ringing the bell, or
more like leaning on it so it kept ringing until I walked to
the front of the house and answered.

"Damn, nigga, you ain't got no patience or what leaning
on my bell like you dying out here?"

"Man, where the fuck my key at, ma? I am not wit'
standing outside waiting on nobody like I am some
creeper or something."

"Whatever. Holla at me when we together for real, and
I will consider a key," I shot back at him while walking to
the table so we could eat.

***

I was sorry I fed his ass so much, because now he had so much energy, and I was tapping out long before him. He had me upside down next to the couch in my bedroom fucking the shit out of me. I couldn't hold on any longer and felt myself have a body-shaking orgasm and then shut it down.

"Damn, girl, you made me sweat. I was working your little ass though," he laughed as he walked to my bed and got in. "I am staying the night. Now let's get some sleep."

"Well, damn, I like how you invite yourself over," I laughed, crawling into bed and lying on top of him. Just like old times, we snuggled in the bed.

Waking up in the morning, the first thing I did was reach for him, but I felt nothing. The house seemed really quiet—too quiet for some reason. Closing my eyes again, a few seconds later I felt a kick to my head that made me fear it was going to be dislodged from my fucking body.

"What the fuck is wrong with you?" I shouted, jumping out of the bed. I could see he had on red Timberland boots, and I suspected that was what he kicked me in the head with. "Nigga, is you fucking crazy? That is my damn head!" I continued to scream while he just stood there looking at me with the meanest look I ever saw on his face. His green eyes were gray almost, and he appeared to be growling at me.

"Yeah, what the fuck is right. So we have a son, one you ran away and hid from me. Oh, yeah, one you have lied to me about all this time you have been back," he yelled in my face as he shoved a picture of Q at me.

"Damn," I said in a low voice.

"Why, Sahnai? What did I do so bad to you that you would run away and hide my only son, shit, only child from me?"

"I never lied. I ran away because of you. I heard you tell Meeka to get rid of y'all baby or you would kill it and her. I overheard you say it more than once to her. She was terrified and so was I, except I was not giving up my baby. He was a part of me and you. I loved you so much and wanted to have your baby. Nothing else mattered, so I took the money I had saved and left," I explained while sobbing.

"Sahnai, I was telling Meeka to get rid of the baby because I only wanted kids with you. I knew you were pregnant, or at least I was pretty sure, and I couldn't have anyone or anything tear us apart or stress you when you were pregnant. You should have come to me, called me, or something. This shit is so selfish of you and unfair to me and our son!

"Yo, have my son here and ready for me to see by five p.m. I gotta get away from you before I strangle you," he yelled as he ran down the stairs and slammed my front door. A few seconds later I could hear the tires hit the pavement as he sped out of my driveway.

Damn, I didn't mean for it to go down like this, but I did feel better now that the secret was out. No more sneaking around with our son.

Chapter 18

Inaya

I had been scared since I lost my job, but God always provides, because I found out the internship with Saber Solutions would be paid. I would still be making more than I was at the day care working three days a week. I started August 1, so I could make it until then. Phantom was nice enough to pay for Kadia to go to summer camp at the YMCA Camp Northpoint as soon as school ended last week. She loved it there. They swam every day, rode horses, and had paint fights. I was grateful because I wouldn't have to worry about a babysitter, and I could start my last semester of school at the end of August with ease. School here didn't start until the first week of September, so I would have been scrambling for two weeks to find somewhere for her to go.

This week being the Fourth of July, camp was closed, and I was in the house with Kadia, bored. She was driving me crazy asking to go to the park, but I was a bit on the tired side this week. I was waiting for Sahnai to come and pick her up so they could swim at her house.

My cell was going off. Phantom was calling me. Every time I heard his voice, I got a tingly feeling in my belly. He really gave me butterflies like he was the first man I had ever met or had sex with.

"Hey, Phantom, what's up?" I asked him.

"Iny, I am about to go see my sister for the Fourth of July for a few days. You and Kades want to come? We gotta leave at like five a.m. though. Think you can be ready by then?"

"Of course we will come with you. Kadia is going swimming with Sahnai, and when she gets back, I will wash her hair and redo her braids. I will pack our clothes while she is gone," I reassured him.

"Okay cool, see you guys tomorrow."

As soon as Kadia closed the door behind her, I got busy. I took a bubble bath and shaved my whole body. Then I grabbed a Guess suitcase for me and a Guess duffel bag for Kadia. She was easy to pack because her clothes and shoes were smaller. I packed my stuff in less than an hour and was even able to finish my laundry.

I did Kadia's hair once she returned. For once she did not fuss because she was excited to go on a vacation, as she called it, with her daddy Phantom. I was excited too. I could barely sleep, and before I knew it, my alarm was alerting me that it was four a.m. Brushing my teeth and taking a shower, I put on black leggings, pink Polo bootie slippers, a white wife-beater, and my denim jacket, and I was ready. I helped Kadia use the bathroom, and then we were outside his door by four forty-five with our bags. I could tell he was happy I was on time. He looked shocked, then smiled at me.

As soon as I got in the car, I took my booties off and propped my feet up on the dashboard while curling up in the seat, trying to get comfortable. Kadia was already back asleep, cuddled up with her Doc McStuffins blanket and her monkey neck pillow.

"Yo, you really put your feet on the dash of my Bentley, ma?" he asked with a smile.

"Yep, and I am about to play a song I'ma sing to you."

Pulling out my iPhone 4S, I connected it to his Bluetooth. While we were waiting for it to sync, he was giving me this look with his lip curled up like he was eating something foul.

"Iny, what the hell kinda phone is that? It look old as hell."

"Phantom, I'm not a baller or dating a baller. It's an iPhone that I am blessed to have because a while ago Sahnai gave it to me when she got the newer one."

"Ma, what carrier you have? Because we going straight to the mobile phone store and get you a real phone. You can give that one to Kadia to play wit'."

"It's T-Mobile if you must know, and my phone is just fine, but if you insist, I will take the new one in rose gold." Hearing my song, "Not Even the King," start to play, I turned it up and started to sing.

"Who sings that song?" he asked me.

"Alicia Keys," I replied, smiling up at him because his hand had moved down and grabbed mine.

"You sing good. You should get in someone's studio or something. The song is a little off though. Who cares about a king?"

"Ha-ha, not really. You have to listen to the song. It's about a woman who loves a man more than any amount of money. She is saying their love is priceless. Listen to the line where she talks about rich people who don't have real friends, just people who hang around them because they have money. It's a deep song. Not as entertaining as 'Trap Queen,' but it has a message."

"That's nice, ma. You really have a different way of looking at the world, and it's a good look."

The ride went by pretty fast, I guessed because we left so early and didn't really catch traffic. I was starting to get nervous about meeting his family. What if they didn't like me? He seemed really close with his sister, and females could be catty.

Pulling up to a huge brick and red house, he backed into the driveway next to a silver Benz truck and a white Porsche Panamera. *Wow, his sister must have a baller too to be living like this.*

Turning to look at me, he said, "Look, ma, before we go in, there are a few things you should know about my sister and my nephews. First off, I have three nephews. The oldest, Cordell, is completely deaf, so he doesn't speak. He is five. The other two boys are Colin and Cazier, who are the three-year-old twins. The last thing is my sister. Her husband died a little over a year ago in a fire. He was a fireman and died saving a kid. She is still hurting from that, but she is really nice. And I know what you're thinking—total opposite of me."

"I am sorry her husband died. That must be hard with three kids all alone. What does she do for work? Her house is huge, and this area seems really nice."

"Ha, my sister has never worked, even though she does have a master's in business. She got a life insurance payout and a settlement from the fire department. Aside from that, she spends my and Lox's money," he laughed.

Again he grabbed Kadia, and I grabbed the bags, and then we walked to the door. As we walked in, he was immediately surrounded by three little boys screaming, hugging, and jumping around everywhere.

"Boys, let your uncle and his guests through the door," I heard his sister say. Stepping inside, we were in a front entryway with benches on either side of a coat closet, so we could sit down and remove our shoes.

"Azia, Cordell, Cazier, Colin, this is my friend Inaya and her daughter, Kadia. Say hello, boys." Before I knew it, I was being hugged by everyone and pulled into the living room. I signed, "Hello, nice to meet you," to Cordell and hugged the twins again. They were at the cute and cuddly age.

"Come on, Inaya, and let me show you where you and Kadia can sleep," Azia said while leading us upstairs with our bags.

I was given a guest room with a huge king-size bed and a fluffy comforter with different shades of blue and browns in it. Looking around, I noticed a chest with a full mirror and a flat-screen smart TV on the wall. The guest bathroom had a tub in it as big as my current bathroom, and marble floors. The shower was separate from the tub, and there was a rain showerhead. I couldn't wait to take a bubble bath.

I was hurt that he introduced me to his sister as his friend, but at least he wasn't cussing me out or telling her I was a bad mother. I would take what I could get with his ol' mean and crazy ass.

"My brother is so rude. If you would like to lie down, go ahead. Kadia will be fine playing with the boys, and you look tired from the drive. By the way, how do you know how to sign?" Azia asked.

"I learned at the day care I used to work in. We had a lot of kids who found it easier to sign instead of speak because they had a disability or speech issue. And thank you, Azia, I am going to lie down if you don't mind."

"Girl, of course not. Get lots of rest, because me and you are going to have so much fun this weekend. Wait until we go shopping," she excitedly said as she walked out of the room, taking Kadia with her.

Lying down, I couldn't help but smile because Azia was so sweet. Soon after Azia left, I felt the bed dip and smelled Phantom's Armani Code as he climbed in behind me, holding me tight until we both fell asleep.

Chapter 19

Phantom

I had to admit, Iny really surprised me on the way down here. Well, really for the whole trip. She fit right in with my sister. They were like two best friends who knew each other forever, and the rest of my family loved her. Most women would have asked if they could spend some of my money by now, and she didn't say a word. Even when Azia invited her to the mall, she said okay and got ready without a word, even though I knew she didn't have any money. Azia was making faces and signing to me that she was the one as soon as she saw that. I still gave her and Azia money, because my sister had no shame in asking for spending money and then some, and I would never let Inaya go shopping with nothing in her pockets. Azia also had no problem asking me to babysit, so now I was sitting here with the boys and Kadia while those two were tearing up the mall.

Cordell came over and signed if he could ask me a question. I nodded yes and waited. "Ha, that was not a question," I signed back, and he laughed. "Yeah, Inaya is pretty, and I am sure she likes you too," I responded. The next thing he signed actually was a question. He asked me if Kadia was my daughter. I guessed I could see the confusion. She clung to me like I was her father, and she had my skin tone and her mother's face. I didn't want to confuse them, but I felt like I was Kades's dad, so I said yes. I made the back-and-forth Y sign, telling him to go play with the other kids.

I didn't know what made me bring Inaya and Kadia with me to my sister's house, but I was not sorry I did. The six-hour drive down went by fast and was full of laughs from both of us. When she wasn't singing to me, she was reading me stuff from her Kindle. That reminded me that I had to pick her up a new phone and an iPad once they got home. Shit, I'd bought Kadia an iPad months ago, and her mom was reading from a black-and-white Kindle. She was too humble. If she had a future with a nigga whose name was big in the streets like mine, she had to step her game up and expect more.

Kadia slept the whole ride. I asked Inaya if she gave her NyQuil or something to knock her out, but she said no, and when I thought about it, leaving at five a.m. was kind of early for a kid. Honestly that was the first thing she did perfectly. I called her and asked if she wanted to go the day before. I told her we were leaving at five, and when they got to my door, their bags were packed and ready, and she had baby girl in some heart PJs and matching slipper-sock things. I carried Kadia, and Inaya grabbed all of our bags, and we were out. She was low maintenance. I expected to have like a two-hour delay once I asked her to come because ladies usually took forever.

On the ride down, she used the bathroom when I stopped and didn't ask me to keep pulling over. Inaya explained that Kadia had on Pull-Ups so she wouldn't wet herself in her sleep. The conversation that followed between us was something great. She was smart. I don't mean like "I can write my name and read a book" smart, which a nigga is lucky if he gets these days with some of these hoes. I mean world smart. She knew politics in the

U.S. and Jamaica. She followed world news and could offer intelligent opinions on the election, the war in Syria, and the slave trade in Africa. Most women I talked to or met couldn't talk about anything but *Love & Hip Hop* and their new yellow weave or plan ways to spend my money that I wasn't giving their asses anyway.

I kept telling her she could sleep if she was tired, and she did that thing where she tilted her head and looked at me like I was crazy. She said she was good keeping me company since I was the driver, and she could take over if I was tired. I had never had a female stay up on the road with me or offer to drive me anywhere.

Hearing the alarm on the door, I went to see what the girls got from shopping. I was used to Azia always showing me all of her purchases. She was usually jumping around like a small puppy, pulling different items out of the bag and walking them in front of my face. After five minutes she'd ask me if I saw it and if I liked it. She had been this way since she was old enough to spend my money in the malls.

"What did you ladies buy with all my money? I'm going to starve next week with all the money I spent on this trip." Once I said that, Iny's face got sad, and she looked like she wanted to fall through the floor or something.

"Girl, please. Don't believe that shit he is saying. He was joking. He is nowhere near starving, and what we just spent was small change. He would have given us more if we'd asked. I don't even ask. I just keep standing there with my hand out until it looks like enough," Azia laughed while pulling more bags in from the garage.

I smiled her way to let her know I was just playing.

"Azia, why you got all those damn Louis Vuitton store bags? Seriously, sell some of this shit you already got, or donate it or something. I just had the purse closet built last March, and I bet it's full already."

"Don't be a spoilsport, Phantom, sheesh. Not all of these bags are mine. Two are for Inaya," Azia responded, rolling her eyes.

"A'ight, Iny. Let's see what you got, ma." It seemed like she made the most of the money I gave her. She had dresses and shorts for her and Kadia from Abercrombie, American Eagle, Burberry, Gucci, and Gap. She had bags of shoes and sneakers from Aldo, Journeys, and the Nike store. Iny had a smile on her face like it was Christmas. She showed me her new Gucci sneakers and her MK watch and accessories. Then came the Louis bag. She was showing all thirty-two when she pulled it out and showed me how it had another little purse inside the tote.

She opened the last Louie bag and took out a box, then handed it to me. She turned to show Kadia her new Burberry dress and matching bows and shoes. Hearing her excited squeals made me feel warm inside. Yeah, she was turning me into a teddy bear instead of a grizzly, but I was only soft for her. I untied the leather bow and pulled back the brown paper to see a red Louis belt and matching shades. I was speechless, because the only females who ever bought me any damn gifts were my sister and my aunt.

"Inaya, come here for a second." I grabbed her and kissed her in front of everyone. I knew I introduced her as a friend to my family, but fuck it, shawty was really starting to get to me. I couldn't imagine life without her. Stepping away from me, she had a grin on her face. I could see my sister standing there and watching us with a look on her face like she was watching a soap opera or some romance movie. *I'm going to make a point to talk to her soon and see what she is thinking.*

"Let's all go to Dave & Buster's our last night here."

The kids were screaming, "Yes!" while running around the kitchen.

"Iny, it's okay to run around like the kids," I teased her. She came up behind me and wrapped her arms around my back.

"Thanks for a great trip," she whispered.

After the kids wore us out at Dave & Buster's, they came home and were knocked right out. Inaya was like a kid too. She and Azia played every game, laughed all night, and she looked so happy and carefree I was almost sad that tomorrow I would have to return her to reality.

I softly knocked on Azia's door before I pushed my way in.

"Ughhh, Jahdair, don't you know how to wait for me to say, 'Come in'? I could have had a man in here or been naked or something for all you knew."

"Girl, you know better than that while I am here. Anyway, what do you think about Inaya and Kades?" I asked. My sister was the most important lady in my life, so her opinion mattered to me.

"Honestly, I love Inaya. She is smart, funny, a good mom, pretty, and most of all, she is head over heels in love wit' your crazy ass. I have no idea why she love your mean ass. Especially how you be cussing her out all the time. Lox told me all about it."

"Tell Lox he needs to shut the fuck up about my personal life. He got enough issues with his runaway ex-girlfriend and their secret son. Oh, yeah, I can see by the look on your face that your news-carrying cousin forgot to mention his newly found son, Lennox Qualyl Hall IV, while you two were over there running down my shit." I already had my phone in hand and pictures pulled up because I knew she would want to see what he looked like.

"Oh, my God, he is so cute. He looks just like Lox. Same ugly ol' green eyes and goofy smile." She went on and on while looking at him.

"That nigga lick his lips just like him, too," I told her, and we both laughed.

"Well, now I have to come and visit soon. The boys will have some time off of camp in August, and we will be popping up on Mr. Lox. I wonder if Dana knows about having a nephew.

"Anyway, back to you and Inaya. I think she is perfect for you, but I know you, and I think you should leave her alone. Kadia thinks you're her dad, and you introduced the woman who loves you as your friend. Don't you see, Jahdair? All you are going to do is hurt her, and she deserves better than that. Plus, she is my friend now, and I don't want you to mess up our friendship."

"Thanks for the pep talk, sis." I leaned over and kissed her on her head as I walked out. "Azia, one last thing."

"Yes, master?"

"No more fucking purses."

Chapter 20

Lox

I was still fucked up over the shit that I found out at Sahnai's house over a week ago. Today was the second time I was going to see my son in person. We were all going to a family day hosted by this local Jamaican restaurant named Royal Palm. The owner, Oscar, was one of my pop's childhood friends, and he did a great job hosting the event every year. There were pony rides and bounce houses for the kids and soccer matches for all ages. The adults could play dominoes or cards, and there were a ton of different foods to choose from.

A part of me was happy I was going to have my son to show off today, even though another part of me was scared he would reject me and cry for his mother. I was so angry I missed out on his first step and first tooth. Hell, his birth was lost to me because of some bitch I cheated with. If I had never told her all that shit . . . hell, let's be honest, if I had never fucked around on Sahnai and had sex with her to begin with, I wouldn't have missed out on my son's beginning. Well, I wasn't going anywhere now. Believe that.

Sahnai is taking too long. I told her to bring him over so he could get dressed here and we could all go together.

I didn't want people to think she was a single mom or anything and try to holler at her with my son. I also wanted to put my junior in the outfit I got him from Saks Fifth Avenue the other day when I was in the city. *He is going to be so fly today, just like his daddy.* I finally heard her loud ass talking to Phantom downstairs, asking if I was ready.

"Yo, bring him up here. I got him some shit to wear," I yelled down the stairs.

She did like I said and didn't dress him in anything but his all-white onesie. I threw the white Burberry shorts and red and checkered Burberry polo shirt on him and then slid the matching plaid Burberry sneakers on his feet. I also put a chain on him. It was of moderate size with a Jesus on the cross and a few diamond chips. Last item was a gold bracelet and some of my Armani Code cologne.

"All right, son, now you and Daddy matching, boy," I said while holding him in my arms. Looking into those green eyes just like mine, I felt like I was looking at a smaller version of me.

"Dada," he said while sticking his drooling finger in my eye.

I could only laugh and say, "Yes. Dada.

"Yo, let's go," I told Sahnai as I popped her on her fat ass. She was lucky she didn't have any clothes here with that little-ass jean-shorts romper she had on over there. Her titties looked like they were going to break out, and her ass looked like it couldn't breathe. If we weren't already running late, she would be going the fuck home and changing.

As soon as I made it to the parking lot, I could see Phantom and Inaya getting Kadia in her booster seat in the back of his truck.

"Yo, Inaya, your cousin left any clothes at your house? Fuck it. Can she wear some of your clothes? Y'all about the same size. Because she got me fucked up walking out the house like that, ass and titties out and shit. As a matter of fact, maybe both of y'all should go change, because that little-ass dress you rocking is not working for me, little sis."

Laughing, Inaya twirled around in her white and pink striped skater dress and matching Guess sandals. "Lox, you are crazy. No one is changing, and me and my cuz are single, you know, like a dollar bill, so we have to look our best. Don't be a hater, because haters get benched."

I couldn't be mad because she was so cute dancing around in her dress with her braids flying in her face.

I could see Phantom smiling at her when he thought no one was looking. I knew she was the one for him. Azia told me all about how he was acting when he took her to Jersey, and even my mom gave me a call about how nice she was. I heard she washed the dishes after dinner. That made my mom fall in love with her. Once I told her that Inaya and Sahnai were cousins, she liked her even more.

Climbing behind the wheel, I smiled, looking over at Sahnai. *This could possibly work. I mean, maybe we could be a family.* I didn't like how Inaya reminded me that they were both still single. I didn't want my son's mother to be single. I wanted her to be here with us, baking cookies and busting it open anytime I wanted. Thinking about how we had sex that last time at her house, I could feel my man rock up and rise in my shorts. *Damn, maybe I can get some after we are done having family time.*

Pulling up at the park, I parked on the grass because I didn't want to hear the ladies whine about walking far.

Finding a table that would fit all of us, we sat down and watched the kids play. Once we all ate some steamed fish and rice, Phantom and I decided to play dominoes.

"Nigga, put your money up and watch me whoop your ass." I talked shit while I started taking these niggas' money.

"Fuck," I heard Phantom say, and this nigga looked like he was trying to hide or some shit. Looking around, I didn't see anyone he could be hiding from. I was almost expecting to see Shawnie again. Turning in my chair, I saw that bitch Tee walking toward us, holding a baby in her arms while her other kids were trailing behind her. *Damn, man, why she got them babies out here looking like that?* No one's hair was combed or cut, their clothes didn't fit properly, and they looked hungry as hell. She had the nerve to be walking around wearing a dress from Bebe and some high-end-looking shoes. *Who the fuck wears high heels to a kids' fun day anyway?* She looked stupid with her feet sinking into the grass and then having to stop and pull them up every few minutes.

She kept walking toward me, and I hoped she was not coming to talk to me. Sahnai was not that stable, and even though we weren't together, there was no telling what she would do, especially if she found out I was fucking this bitch.

"Phantom, you think you can fuck me and leave me alone? Nigga, you don't see my phone calls and text messages?" Tee said as she walked up to the table with her hand on her hip. Everybody who was in our area started staring and watching to see the drama. I just stayed quiet trying to figure out if this bitch was really fucking me and my cousin. I mean, come on, she knew what the fuck she was doing, because people knew us everywhere we went.

"Phantom, I texted you and told you I am pregnant, and I get nothing, right?" she yelled as she threw the ultrasound picture at him.

I was not sure she really understood my cousin, or she would have rethought this whole situation. Before anyone could react or notice, this crazy nigga jumped up from the table and punched her dead in her face while she was holding the baby and all.

"Toya, fuck you. Bitch, I wouldn't run in that rotten pussy raw if it were the last pussy on earth. Now shut up with that bullshit and go find your baby daddy."

Like a light bulb went off, she finally noticed me sitting at the table, and a smile crawled across her dumb-ass face.

"Tee, for real, ma, you fucking me and my cousin? What, you got community pussy? Don't say a fucking word to me, you nasty bitch." *Wow, I can't believe Tee is Toya. What a small fucking world.*

"I wasn't a nasty bitch when I was sucking your dick last week. And surprise, nigga, I wasn't no nasty bitch when me and you had this fucking baby, pussy," she shouted while damn near throwing her baby at me and turning to walk away. I looked up to see Inaya and Sahnai just watching to see what I was going to do.

"Yo, Tee, come get your kid, man. You putting on a whole fucking show for these people out here because you want some attention. You want everybody to know you was smashin' the 'niggas' in the street? A'ight, you got that."

I stood up and went to go give this girl back her baby, but when I looked down to make sure I was holding him securely, I noticed his eyes. *Fuck.* Even though I couldn't see his face under all the dirt that was caked on and the scabs that were covering his cheeks, his eyes were looking back at me, shining a bright green. I had never been this angry in my life. It was no way like how I felt when I found out about Q. When I finally found out about him, he was well taken care of. Hell, even though my mom didn't want to tell me, I realized she and my pops had seen and known about him.

This shit right here didn't make any sense. Toya stopped for one second and looked like she wanted to walk back, but now that I knew he was my son, that bitch was straight up out of luck. *She better not even come back over here, because she straight up won't make it.* Instead of coming too close, she threw a manila envelope in my direction and started walking away again, slowly, with her heels still getting stuck in the grass and dirt.

As soon as Sahnai walked over to me and looked at the baby's face with the red welts and scabs, I realized that Toya or Tee or whoever the fuck she was had better walk a little faster.

"Hey, Toya, so that's it, bitch? You come over here and announce that you fucking my man and my cousin's man, and then you leave his baby he didn't even know about without a care?"

Once she heard her name, she stopped and turned around like she had done nothing wrong. "If you was his woman, he wouldn't be in my bed every week now, would he? It's his turn now to deal with that bastard baby. His little ass is always sick, always crying and shit. My daughter cannot manage to take care of him, and I am busy. I have a life, you know."

Just like I knew, Sahnai was on her like white on rice. There was blood everywhere, and when she was done, Toya's shoes were broken from Sahnai hitting her in the face with them. The odd thing was that Toya's other two kids never cried out or reached for her. They did not even look fazed, like this happened every day. My heart went out to them, but since they were not mine, there was nothing to do. I didn't even know what to do with this baby or how to care for him. I wished Sahnai would have saved the drama for another day. Right now her focus should have been on these kids out here, including our son. Like always, she had to show her ass no matter who was watching.

Once Toya finished limping away toward the parking lot, I realized I had a dirty baby with no clothes or bottles. Hell, I didn't even know his age or name. Looking around for Sahnai to come help, I could see her staring at me like she wanted to kill me. Fuck, I didn't know about this kid. It wasn't my fault, so if Sahnai couldn't get on board, fuck her. *Now she want to be mad and shit after she basically did the same fucking thing with Q. He is still my son, and I'm not about to keep letting him be abused. That's Sah's problem now. She can't communicate. She's always mad or scared or hurt but don't say shit unless she is lashing out in a fight. I am twenty-four and have two kids. I don't have time for kiddie games. Hell, at twenty-one I would have thought she would have grown the fuck up by now.*

Inaya interrupted my thoughts. "His name is Aiden, and he is four months old. There is a baby store only ten minutes away. Let me go and grab some stuff for him. Take him home, and we can clean him up and feed him. I will help if you need help. It will be okay," she said while giving me a half hug and running her hand over the baby's curly hair.

See, little sis was the shit. I could tell she was hurt by what Phantom did, especially knowing the girl could be carrying his baby, but she focused on the important thing here: my innocent son who was suffering. Not cussing out her man or fighting a broke-down bum bitch.

"Iny, take my credit card and my truck. I will ride with Phantom and get the kids home. Oh, and, sis, I appreciate you rocking wit' me, because this shit is fucking my head up bad."

Walking to my truck, I noticed Sahnai stop and kick it with Phine for a few minutes. That nigga handed her some bread, and she put it in her Michael Kors bag and followed Inaya to my truck. *Good. I don't want to be around her right now anyway. Fuck her. Then she still got the nerve to be all in Phine's face. Now I have to beef with my li'l nigga because she is a fucking thot.*

Two hours later I got a text from Naya asking for help. Walking outside, I saw her dragging boxes out of the back of the truck, and bags were touching the ceiling of the Range. *Well, damn, good thing the Black Card has no limit.* I was sure that Amex would be giving me a possible fraud call soon.

"What the fuck you buy, the whole baby store?" I asked while raising my eyebrows.

"Babies need a lot of stuff. A thank-you would be nice," replied Sahnai. I should have known her shopaholic self was the one who had a hand in this.

As soon as we got everything in the house, I felt like I should leave. We set up just the basics, since I didn't even know what room little man would have yet or what to do with him. Inaya was going to keep him until I could figure it out. As I was leaving so I could get some air, I heard Sahnai bathing him and then singing to him as she walked him around the room.

Before I could make it out the door, she made her way downstairs to me with Aiden in her arms. It looked like she would be the one caring for him and not Inaya. I wasn't going to acknowledge it because I was still mad at her and her bullshit.

I walked out the door feeling a little better. Li'l man was cooing and drinking a fresh bottle. His body was all clean and medicine had been put on his face and he had on a little sleeper with green, orange, and blue stripes. He looked so cute in Sahnai's arms while she rocked him back and forth. I slowly let the door close behind me.

Chapter 21

Inaya

I had not seen Phantom in over two weeks, ever since we got in an argument about him accusing me of sleeping with my professor, Mr. Thomas. See, like always, Phantom's mean, woman-hating ass thought the worst of me and didn't care who knew it. He called me a whore in front of the whole class, threatened to kill me if I gave him any diseases from sleeping with the professor, and then threatened Mr. Thomas. He told him that if he didn't stay away from me, he would rip out his tongue and his eyes. He was so mad it looked like foam was coming out of his mouth, and his coal black eyes turned a shade darker, if possible. All of this nonsense just because I came to class early to go over my final project with Professor Thomas, and I guessed because he was black we got to be fucking? I mean, damn, he was almost 40 years old. I could have been his daughter.

I was so embarrassed I thought about never going back to school again, but I just decided on never going back to Mr. Thomas's linguistics class. I had been e-mailing him the assignments and homework since then, and if he failed me, oh, well. I would retake it next term with a different teacher. I was too ashamed to face him again all because Phantom was a fucking nut. He only showed his behind like a spoiled, angry child because he wanted to push me away. I saw through his actions now. I wished I had what it took to break through his many layers of pain and distrust, but I didn't. I was not superwoman, and I was not in possession of a magic wand, so I was ready to give up.

As I jumped up and ran to the bathroom just in time, I could feel the bile burn my nose and throat as it made its way out. So there was this. I had been throwing up for a few days now. At first I thought it was a bug, and honestly, I only went to the doctor because I was feeling a pain in my lower back. After sitting in the emergency room for almost five hours, assuming I was having kidney failure or appendicitis (thanks, WebMD), the nurse came in with a big ol' clown smile on her face. That was when I noticed the little square white plastic test in her hand. My mind was screaming, *nooooo,* but my heart was beating yes. I was still hurt about him having a baby on the way with that bitch Toya. Now we both were gonna have his baby, I guessed. This made the situation more stressful.

As soon as she told me I was pregnant, a part of me was happy. If I couldn't have the man I loved, I would at least have a part of him. I saw him come in last night, so I decided that this morning would be the day I told him. No matter how he felt, he deserved to know about his baby. Shit, I was learning from Sahnai's mistakes. I thought Lox was going to kill her when he found out she never told him about his son. There was no denying who Q's daddy was with those green eyes and long eyelashes. They could have been twins. They even licked their lips the same way. That must be some light-skinned nigga shit, because I'd never seen men do that out of habit the way they did. At first I thought she just wasn't feeding his little ass enough and he was hungry or something.

I decided to throw on a sweat suit since it was kind of chilly out today. We had been lucky that the weather had been holding steady in September. I pulled the matching white and gold Victoria's Secret Pink hoodie over my head and slid my feet into my all-white Jordan slides. I brushed my hair out of its wrap and brushed my teeth again. After gargling with mouthwash and throwing on my Tiffany heart earrings and necklace that Phantom bought me and a pair of Gucci shades, I felt like I looked good considering this baby was kicking my ass.

I know this is the right thing to do. Phantom is not like Noah. Even though he had not been to see me in two weeks, he had picked up Kadia from school and taken her to dinner several times. On Wednesday, when they had their soccer games, he had Lox knock on the door and grab her so she could watch him, and he deposited $2,000 in my account every week without a word, just like before. Every time I put up a fight about the money, he told me it was so Kadia was straight.

Honestly, I didn't even touch half the money. He paid the light bill monthly and left a credit and did the same with my cell phone and rent. Plus, he always took Kadia with him to the mall or he and Lox were bringing bags filled with clothes. I thought often about how much my life had changed in less than a year.

I had been meaning to buy a cheap car, but somehow I was always being picked up and dropped off by Phantom or driving his bimmer or Audi around. He had shown me his love in so many ways. He just didn't know how to say it. He would be a great dad. I wondered if I was talking myself into this. *Maybe I should get an abortion or just not tell him. You know what, forget it. I am just going to get this over with, then go buy a milkshake.* I had been wanting milkshakes every day with this kid.

As soon as I closed my door, I saw Phantom's door open. *Good, I can catch him on his way out.* Lox was at Sahnai's house. I didn't think she would ever get away from him now. He wouldn't be letting her go anywhere with his son. Instead of Phantom's head, I saw a female step out. She was average at best: long, curly weave, brown skin, a flat ass, her nose looked like it belonged to a pug, and on her feet she had some wedge sandals with crusty toes peeping out. I'd recognize that hand slapping her ass anywhere. The tattoo of a dragon jumped out and caught my eye. *I guess I won't be telling Phantom right now, maybe not at all. He seems to be preoccupied.*

Quickly walking by the two, I made sure to hold my head up high and not let a tear fall even though being pregnant had my hormones all over the place. As soon as I walked into IHOP, I sat down and ordered my milkshake first. Feeling my phone vibrate in my purse, I dug it out, a small part of me hoping it was Phantom sending me an apology. Another part of me wanted to tell him where to shove his dirty dick.

Unknown: Bitch, I finally found you. I bet you thought you could run away from me, but I will never let you go. You thought I wouldn't get a visa to come to the U.S.? To think all along you were only a few hours away from me. That was clever of you. Pretty soon I will have you both back in Canada with me where you belong. You thought you could take my little girl from her daddy? That will never happen. She needs me to punish her daily. I can see you are not giving her the proper punishments. She looks too happy. I seen you and her at the park last week. Oh, and don't think that big-time nigga you fucking wit' will save either one of you. Shit, he was getting head in the bathroom from another bitch while you were pushing Kadia on the swings. Inaya, no one will ever want you. You and Kadia are damaged goods. I am coming for you!

Oh, my God, Noah found us! I don't know how. I was careful when I left. I could feel my palms sweat and my heart race. I thought I was going to pass out right in the IHOP, but somehow I made my way to my car and blindly drove home. I made it home and texted Sahnai, telling her what happened and asking her if she could keep Kadia a few days until I figured out what to do next. She agreed.

After making some tea and turning the phone off, I stripped down to my bra and panties and threw myself on my all-white Polo comforter. Pressing play on Netflix and cuddling up close to my pillow, I let the sounds of the TV lull me to sleep.

Chapter 22

Lox

Looking out at the glistening pond and listening to the boys make noise on the baby monitor, I knew I had to talk to Sahnai today. It wasn't that I didn't still love her, but thinking about what Phine and JRock said about her and the stares she got everywhere we went in public, I felt like everyone knew how she was or she had talked to every guy who glanced her way. She said she wasn't sleeping with any of them, but could I really believe that? I knew myself, and I couldn't handle her the way she was.

Her messing around with all of these dudes, taking their money and stuff, made me feel like less of a man. I wanted to be the one to provide for her. I mean, she had my first son. She shouldn't have to struggle at all. I had more than enough money to take care of her, but she was still in the streets, going on dates, and chatting up different men, allowing them to take her shopping or pay her bills. Aside from me, she could get a job or something. I knew how smart she was, and sitting around doing nothing all day was not cute at all. Even Inaya went to school and had an internship with a good company. I wished she could behave more like her or the old Sahnai I remembered.

She still looked the same though: pretty, round baby face, bright eyes, and a banging body. Her hair was different now that it was blond, and she cut it, but it suited her. Hell, the pussy still felt the same too. Nah, fuck it. The pussy felt better than it used to. I guessed the older she got, the more tricks she learned or something.

Getting the kids dressed, I felt bad about letting go of Q's mom and the only good mom Aiden had ever known. I grew up with both of my parents, so I didn't want them to be without both of us. I also didn't want them to grow up in a house where we were both fighting all the time because I couldn't trust their mom. I was making this decision for them too. Yep, this was the best. We had had too much drama lately, and it was time to make it stop. As soon as I had this talk with Sahnai, I was going to suggest a family vacation. I would have Inaya and Kadia come, and she and her cousin could share a suite with the kids, and I could have my own room to chill in.

Texting Sahnai, I told her to meet us at the park so Q could play and the baby could get some fresh air. Looking at all the messages I had, I could see about twenty were from Toya's ratchet ass. Now she was claiming that the new baby she was carrying could be mine and not Phantom's. I didn't have shit to say to this bitch after how she treated my son and she kept him from me. For what? He was not light skinned like Q, but once she saw the green eyes, she should have known he was mine. Now she was saying we could get married and be together as a family. She was crazy. I never led her on and told her I wanted to be with her, even before I found out about Aiden.

Shaking my head at the foolishness of this bitch, I grabbed Q's hand and Aiden's baby seat and headed to the car. As soon as I got there, I realized I left the baby bag in the house. "Fuck."

"Fuck," Q repeated.

"No, Qualyl, don't say that. Only Daddy can say that," I told him with my serious daddy face on. I was hoping he wouldn't cry, and lucky for me, he just laughed and went back to pulling away from me, trying to run toward a ball one of the kids left outside. Walking back to the house and trying to open the door while holding two kids was not easy.

Grabbing the cream and white Gucci diaper bag Sahnai bought for both boys to use, I then struggled back out the door with one more thing to carry. After getting Q strapped into the car seat and turning Aiden's seat around about fifteen times, I finally heard a click and thanked God he was in there securely. *I don't know how Sahnai does this, especially with two kids. She makes it look effortless.*

Pulling up, I parked, and Sahnai ran over to the car and grabbed Aiden out of the baby seat first and then grabbed Q out. She began kissing Aiden's face like she had not seen him in a year, even though it was only a night.

"Look at my baby. Yes, that's you, my baby," she began talking to him like I wasn't even standing there. "Dang, Lox, I thought you wasn't coming. What took so long?" she scolded me, grabbing the baby bag and walking toward the park.

"Yo, that fancy-ass European car seat you bought Aiden that cost a fortune doesn't work right. It took me like twenty minutes to figure out how the seat fits in there. I think that shit is broke, ma."

I swore she was laughing so hard tears were rolling down her face, and she couldn't catch her breath. "Well, let me inform you of a few things. One, the seat is not broken at all. Two, you did not get it on the base right. My baby was in there backward and shit. And last, this shit was not expensive. I'ma show you how it's done when we leave here."

I followed her over to the swings, and she put the baby in the stroller she had ready and waiting when we got there and handed him a toy. Honestly, I was just glad I didn't have to try to work the fucking stroller. It looked like some futuristic shit. It was not even like a normal stroller. It sat the baby way up in the air, and the handle was shaped like an eye or some shit. I remembered when we bought it the people at the store couldn't even figure out how to work it. It was called a Stokaya or Stokayke or some shit. Even though it cost over a grip and I complained at the store, Aiden looked happy in it, and I wanted the best for my kids, so I really didn't care about spending the money. I just liked fucking with Sahnai about what she spent, especially when it came to my babies.

She pushed Q on the swing for a while, then moved to the kiddie slides and let him go. For 2 years old my li'l man was smart. He was climbing the stairs and sliding down on his own. I guessed it was now or never.

"Sah, can we talk for a few minutes?"

"What's up, Lox? You okay? Toya isn't trying to get Aiden back, is she?" she said with a worried look on her face. She unconsciously moved closer to Aiden and put her hand on him in the stroller. See, those were the reasons I loved her, but this shit just wouldn't work.

"Look, Sahnai, I will always have love for you. I mean, we have a kid together, and I was an asshole when I asked Inaya to help with Aiden instead of you. I mean, yeah, that was some petty shit, and I know it hurt you. I am sorry for that, ma. You like his mom now, and I am blessed that you are here to raise our kids, and you doing a great job. I want to talk to you about a few things. First, I want to buy you a house for you and the kids. They need a yard to run around in and all that shit. I know Q loves the water and, hell, so does little princess Kades."

I could see her body relax as we grabbed Q and started walking to the cars.

"Okay, that seems like a good idea. I feel guilty allowing you to spend so much on me, but since it's for the good of the kids, I guess it's okay. I appreciate it from the bottom of my heart. And for the record, Lox, I never stopped loving you. I should have confronted you when I overheard the conversation wit' you and Meeka, but I was scared. I know it's no excuse, but it is the truth."

"Ma, I understand why you did what you did and ran away. I mean, you loved me that much that you couldn't allow anything to happen to my seed, and I respect it. I know you used to doing you now, and I know you not bringing no niggas around the boys, but I want to give you an allowance. I don't want you to feel you have to keep finding some baller to support you, ma. None of these niggas got money like me, and you my only baby moms, so I have to make sure you straight. I'ma pay the house bills and give you five grand in cash a month. Also, we need to pick out a new whip. That little car ain't gonna make it in the winter, so you need a truck. I got a Black Card on its way with your name on it for when you buy food and the kids need shit. I mean you too, ma. If you need some clothes or a bag to make you feel good, go for it. You not supposed to struggle, ya hear me?"

"A'ight. Is that all? You made it seem like this was something bad, had a bitch shaking inside," she laughed nervously. "Let me show you how to put this seat in properly."

In two seconds, she shoved the seat on the base in her car with the baby facing the back seat. I could see the smirk on her face, and I had to admit, she got that one. Grabbing her hand, I leaned in to kiss her one last time.

"Look, Sahnai, I want you to know I got love for you, but I am not in love with you anymore. This is not about all the bullshit with you running away or even you lying about Q. I just can't mess with a girl like you. It would drive me crazy to always wonder what guy you slept with or which one of my friends you went on a few dates with to get some bands out of. I mean, shit, I really don't know what you doing wit' these niggas, ma. So it's best if we just part ways."

"What the fuck you mean a girl like me?" she asked in a voice that sounded way too calm to me. So I decided to answer carefully.

"You know, a girl with a reputation," I replied. I opened the driver door for her to get in and turned to walk to my car. My stomach hurt knowing the kind of pain I just caused the woman I was still truly in love with, but again, a nigga was doing what was best for all of us. We had kids and didn't need to be distracted with all of this back and forth, rumors, and arguments kind of shit.

As I turned around to make sure she got in her car all right, I noticed she was kneeling on the ground hunched over. *Damn, I may have to get her and the kids home so she can cry it out there. Maybe I will drop them off at Grams's. She will be all right in a few days.*

"Yo, Sah, come on, ma. Get up. We gotta get the kids home. They need to eat," I called out as I jogged up to her. She lifted up her head, and instead of the tears I expected to see, her eyes were glassy, like she'd just smoked a pound and was about to pass out. That was when I noticed the blood dripping next to the car. Pulling her in my arms, I noticed that she had open wounds in her stomach and side.

"Sahnai, what the fuck happened, ma?" I yelled in her face as I took off my T-shirt to try to stop the blood. Picking up the phone with shaky hands, I dialed 911.

"911, what's your emergency?"

"I am at Powder Mills Park, and my girl has been stabbed or something. Send an ambulance right away," I told the operator before I dropped the phone on the concrete and held her close to my heart.

Who the fuck would do this to her? I only turned my back for a minute. My mind was going a hundred miles an hour, and what seemed like hours later, I heard the sirens in the distance. *What if she doesn't make it?* The last thing I said to her was that I wasn't in love with her anymore.

Chapter 23

Phantom

"Look, Iny, I know you are not going to agree with this one bit, but I need you to hear me out. Especially with everything that happened with Lox. I feel like I made a good decision for Kades today," I started as soon as I picked her up from work.

"Jah, I trust you with Kadia. As much as I don't trust anything else about you, I know you would never hurt Kades. She means the world to you for whatever reason, and I respect that." With that said, she turned up the radio and began singing that song "Almost" by Tamia.

Damn, her voice sounded so sad. She sounded that way because of me. I knew it seemed like I was playing with shawty's emotions. This was why I wanted to just be friends and I had no intentions of fucking her. I could tell she was in love with me, but I couldn't let another woman into my heart. It was just too hard, and I was not up for it. I felt like I needed to say something, maybe something to make this easier. *She must know that I am pulling away from her.* I hadn't slept with her in a few weeks, and she saw Kadaja leaving my house early this morning when she left for work. I bet that was why she didn't ask me for a ride and got her stubborn behind on the bus. I bet she was thinking about it right now, and that was why tears were creeping down her cheeks. *My little crybaby. She cries for everything, but it's cute to me.* It let me know she had real feelings.

She would be straight, though, because on Saturday her new whip would be ready. I wanted to make sure she was straight before I ended whatever this was, so I copped her a brand-new black-on-black 2016 Cadillac truck. I made sure it was fully loaded and had those TVs in the headrest for my baby girl. I even had the dealership cop the safest booster seat so Kades was safe when her speed demon mama was behind the wheel. I still remembered the time I let her drive my Bentley. I was holding on to the door, and she was taking corners like the Indie 500. She scared the piss out of me that day, but she was a rider for real. When we went back to Brooklyn, she drove there and back, and we made the seven-hour drive in a little under five.

If I could choose a girl to fall in love with, it would be her. Her smile and her laugh when she was happy just made me want to smile. It felt like a bottle of sunshine opened up even when it was a bad day, when everything was going wrong. I loved how she fought her sleep like one of the kids and slept with the TV on because she was scared of the dark. Once she finally got there, she poked her feet out of the bottom of the covers and curled up close to my back like a baby. *I'ma miss that. She is my comfort, but I am her heartbreak.*

"Jah, where are we going?" she asked with her face turned to the window. I guessed she was trying to hide her tears even though I could hear them in her voice and see them in her reflection. I realized we had just been driving around. I didn't have any real destination in mind. How do you pick a place to tell someone you are ending things with them? It wasn't like they had a special restaurant just for breakups. Her head was tilted to the side while she waited for me to answer.

"Let's go walk on the beach. We can get ice cream or summin', unless you're hungry. We can go eat."

"The beach is fine."

Once we pulled up, I walked her to the Abbott's, and we waited in line. I couldn't help but smile as I remembered the first time we had ice cream together. Kades, her, and me. In a different world they would be my family. I would go to work and come home to Iny and maybe even have more kids with her. I wished I were there when she was pregnant with Kades. I would have rubbed her feet and fed her anything she wanted. See, this was what I meant. *She got a nigga soft as a bitch.*

After we finished our cones, I led her down to the sand. She slipped her heels off and held them in one hand and slipped her other hand into mine. I could feel her tiny fingers gripping mine, like if she held on to me tight enough, I would stay.

"Look, Iny, I don't know how to start this. A nigga like me is no good with words. I am not the type to give a fuck about people's feelings, but you and Kades came around and changed all of that." I paused to run my hand over my braids. It's something I did when I was stressed or didn't know what to do next. Iny made me realize I could love, but I was afraid of that love. I was not into settling down with one female or even respecting one. That was obvious by the shit I was saying to Inaya.

"I can't do this anymore, whatever this is. I am going to be on the road a lot more now, and I don't want to. Really it's just not fair for you to wait around for me. I am not the one for you, ma. I keep hurting you, and it will never end. I can't be the man you want or you need. We will always be friends, and I always got your back, and Kadia, she will always be my little girl. I got you guys a new truck, and it will be delivered tomorrow. I put extra funds in your account, and the bills are paid for the next few months. If you need anything, ma, just ask Lox. He will get a message to me."

She wasn't saying a word, but I could see her shoulders shaking, and her white blouse was see-through with the tears that were raining from her eyes. I walked over and pulled her close, letting her tears wet my Armani T-shirt.

"What about Kadia? She will be crushed. You became a father figure to her, and now you are walking away. She didn't deserve this," she cried out as she turned to walk closer to the water. "Phantom, there is something I need to talk to you abo—" She stopped short when she looked at a message on her phone. Her face turned pale, and she was suddenly shaking.

"What is wrong, Iny? Talk to me."

"Phantom, where is Kadia? She is home with Lox, right? Or did Sahnai pick her up?"

"Iny, that's what I have been meaning to talk to you about. Noah reached out to me a while back. I understand he used to put his hands on you, and you did right by running away from him, but you cannot keep a man from his child just for that. After I watched how hurt Lox was missing out on Q's life, I figured it would be a good idea to let Kadia spend some time with Noah. She is visiting with him until later on." Her face looked like someone was dying in front of us. It was a mix of horror and sadness.

"Babes, look, you don't have to deal with him at all. He can drop her off and pick her up from Sahnai. I already told him to not mess wit' you and just focus on his kid. Ma, no matter what, you was wrong for keeping him from his kid. He is a loving father and deserves better than that."

"Phantom, you have no idea what you have done. You let your low judgment of me cost both of us the person we love the most. I told you over and over again Kadia cannot be around her father, and that's why we ran away. I never said he put his hands on me or that I was mad at him. Phantom, he was hurting Kadia, physically and regularly. You just gave my daughter to a monster," she screamed before she ran toward the car.

Chapter 24

Kadia

I'm scared.

I was supposed to go home on Sunday, but my dad
kept me here. This house was not like home. It was dirty
and dark. When I looked around, there were dishes with
food stuck to them all over, and the floors were sticky.
The walls had red drops running down them like someone threw juice and never wiped it up. I had to sleep on
an old couch. It was green and smelled funny, like how
people smell who live on the street. At night I wrapped
up in my princess blanket I brought from home. It was
pink and blue and purple, all my favorite colors, and it
smelled like Mommy's perfume and soap and a little like
Daddy Phantom. He always smelled good. I wondered
why Phantom made me go with my real dad. I wished
Phantom were my real dad, because Noah was so mean
to me. I didn't think he knew my dad used to hurt me, or
he wouldn't have made me go. Once, when I was playing
at the park, a bigger boy ran by and knocked me down,
and Phantom yelled at him so much he made the boy run
away crying. I wished he were here to make my dad
run away crying too. Phantom told me I would only be
with Noah until Sunday, but now it was Wednesday, and

he had not picked me up. I asked my dad every day if I could call Mommy or Phantom, but he just laughed and told me Mommy would be coming soon and would be with me. If I asked too many times, he hit me with the back of his hand or pinched my arms and legs. It hurt so bad I couldn't help but cry.

I didn't know if my mommy was coming for me. I knew he used to hurt her too, and that was why we ran away. I thought my mom believed I didn't remember when my dad used to hurt me, but I did. He would punish me for everything, and that was how I learned to be so quiet. If I was quiet, then maybe he wouldn't notice me and wouldn't yell or punish me. I wondered why my daddy hated me. I didn't make a mess, and I did well in school. He was mean for no reason. This time was really bad, worse than before when Mommy was around. I didn't have a bed to sleep in or food to eat, and no one was washing my clothes or brushing my hair. I wished I could run away, but I couldn't get out because he locked me in. When he left, he put me in the closet and locked the door. Sometimes I heard him come in, and I heard a woman's voice. They laughed and made funny noises, and then the woman would leave, and he would let me out. I was happy when I was in the closet. He let me have my princess blanket. While I was in there, I remembered what Mommy said about God seeing everything and always being there for me. I knew Mommy was right, so I had been praying every day and night. I wanted to be home with my mommy and Phantom and my cousins.

Every time I thought being with my dad was bad, I didn't realize how much worse it could get, until yesterday. The same as every day since I had been there, I woke up to Noah throwing cold water on me and yelling for me to get up. Then he grabbed me by my arms and twirled me around, then let go. I hit the wall and then dropped to the floor with a thud. This made my dad laugh. I didn't think that it was funny or understand why it would make him laugh. I never did anything to him, but he thought it was funny to hurt me. After he gave me a cup of water and some dry cereal, I heard a car pull up. I was so happy. I thought finally Phantom had come to get me. Instead, she came. She was awful. She walked in and kissed Daddy on his lips, and I thought that was strange because it was his mommy, and I didn't think that was how you kissed your mommy.

I still remembered her, my grandma from before when we lived with Noah in Canada. She was mean. She always made Mommy cry. She would walk in with her big fur coat on and her really red lipstick. It was all over and around her lips. It looked like I put it on her. Even though her makeup looked funny, she was mean. I could see it in her eyes when she looked at us. Her eyes were like the evil people in *Snow White* and *101 Dalmatians*. Before she left, my dad shoved me toward her and never said a word, just left the room laughing some more. She dragged me to the car, and now I was here.

I had been here two days now. I counted on my fingers. At least Grandma's house was clean and there was a bed. There were also clean clothes, but they were not mine. They looked old and were scratchy. Grandma kept calling me Tameka and yelling at me for sitting in Daddy's lap too long or for playing with Noah's toys. I didn't know why I would play with my daddy's toys. I didn't even think he had toys. He was a grown-up. Today she called someone on the phone and told her to bring her granddaughter over because she missed her and wanted her to meet her sister.

I didn't know who she was talking about, because I didn't have a sister. I wanted a sister someday. I wanted Mommy and Phantom to have a baby when I got home so I could have someone to play with. *I really want to go home now.*

"Tameka," my grandmother yelled. The first time she called me that name, I tried to tell her my name was Kadia, but she made me kneel on metal bottle caps for hours after that, so now I answered no matter what name she was calling me. Whoever Tameka was must have really made my grandma mad, because when she thought I was her, she was twice as mean.

"Yes, ma'am," I quickly replied.

"Come and get dressed. We have company coming over, and you better behave and not cry about wanting to go home to your mommy. I am your mommy now, and if you don't listen, I will get rid of you like I should have to begin with."

She gave me a bath next, but the water was so hot my skin started to peel.

"Owww!" I couldn't help it and cried out as she began scrubbing me with a rough washrag and some smelly black soap.

"Shut up," she yelled and pushed me deeper into the boiling hot water. She put some old-lady-smelling lotion on my skin that smelled like mints, and it burned. Then she put a red dress on me with white lace, and it hurt my skin. Before I could say anything, I heard someone lightly knocking on the door.

"Lallani, go in the other room and see your sister. Kadia, come down here." An older girl who was pretty and looked a lot like me came into the living room.

"OMG, Kadia, are you okay?" she whispered. I just shook my head, afraid that my grandma would hear and come punish me some more. My sister played with me until her mommy said it was time to go. I thought I saw my sister and her mommy at the park one day. I thought Daddy Phantom hit her mommy and made her cry. My sister's mommy hugged me and whispered in my ear that they would get me home to my mommy soon. I hoped she would help me. *I miss my mommy.*

Chapter 25

Lox

I woke up to the steady beep of the machine in Sahnai's hospital room and the eerie green glow from all the machines she was hooked up to. It'd been this way for over a week. She survived the stabbing in the park with some internal bleeding and trauma to her spleen. The doctors said she would make a full recovery once she woke up, if she woke up. They said she was still out of it due to the lack of blood and trauma to her body, and it was more about her will to wake up than the state of her physical body.

Between me taking care of the kids basically alone and hitting the streets trying to find Kadia and waiting on Sahnai to wake up, I was exhausted both physically and mentally. I had also been on the hunt for Toya's snake ass. I felt like she had something to do with this. I couldn't think of anyone else who would want to hurt Sahnai. So this shit really felt like my fault, and once I handled Toya and Sahnai was good, I thought it was best for me to still just be her baby daddy. Not because I didn't love her or want to be with her, but I didn't want my past to start catching up to both of us, and for the sake of our son, I had to put their safety before my happiness.

Thank God for Inaya and Sahnai's grandmother and little cousin helping me out with the kids. Walking over and kissing Sahnai on the cheek, I whispered in her ear, "I love you," and walked out. I had a lot of shit to get done today. Azia and her kids were coming soon, and I wanted my mom to come down and help me with the boys, so I decided to look into a house. I couldn't keep us all in this tiny townhouse, so I was meeting with someone today in the gated community around the corner called the Reserve. I was really just looking for something new, big, and ready to buy now.

Pulling up and seeing the real estate lady pacing in front of her little blue Toyota Prius, I got out with a laugh. She saw me and gave me the "damn, you fine" smile, but I made sure to give her a frown. I mean, she was cute for a white girl, even had little dimples and shit, but I remembered the last time I said a white girl was cute, I ended up tied up and being raped and shit. Plus, I would hate to have to body my real estate agent.

"Hello, Mr. Hall," she greeted me, shaking my hand and opening the front door of a brownstone house. "This is a four-bedroom home. On the ground floor there is a playroom, office, dining room, eat-in kitchen, and a bathroom. Please look around and let me know what you think." She finished her little speech with a big-ass smile and popped her chest out.

Looking around, I honestly didn't even know what I was looking for. I mean, as long as the kids had a playroom and the yard was fenced in, I was good. The bedrooms looked big, and the kids would all be on the same floor as me, so I was cool with it.

"Yo, I will take it. I need to move in ASAP because I have two kids and they need more space to move around in." As I spoke, Becky or whatever her name was had a huge grin on her face while handing me a pen and some paperwork.

"Here you are, Mr. Hall. I hope you enjoy your home, and on behalf of Nothnagle Realty, we would like to thank you for being a client. If you ever need anything, and I mean anything, you have my number," she said as she handed me the keys to the house and winked before switching out the front door.

Shit, I wished Sahnai was up and doing right so she could help me decorate this shit. Knowing that Inaya would help, even though she was going crazy without Kadia, I picked up the phone and called her up.

"Yo, little sis, what's up? You hanging in there?" I asked with concern.

"Hey, Lox. Yeah, I am trying my best. I feel like I am losing my mind without my baby." I could hear her voice cracking like she wanted to cry and shit. I couldn't blame her. Now that I had kids, I couldn't fucking imagine something going on with one of my little ones, especially some shit where I couldn't see or find them. I didn't know what the fuck my cousin was thinking, but he fucked up on this one big time.

"How is Sahnai today? I have not had a chance to get up there yet since I am not feeling so hot."

"She is doing the same. The doctors say it is just a matter of time and she should be up soon. You don't worry about Sahnai. I got her. Just take care of yourself so you a hunnit when baby girl gets home. And, Inaya, we will make sure she gets home. I promise you that." Even as I said it, I hoped I could keep my promise. I didn't know anything about this enemy yet, so I felt like I was walking around blind.

"Lox, I trust you, not Phantom's ass, but I trust you. I know you mean what you say. You standing by my cousin's side after all that has happened and stepped up to take care of both kids on your own. You're a good guy, and I hope my cousin doesn't let you get away, because

I ain't approving no new boyfriends or cuddle buddies, whatever she want to call them." The last part made us both laugh a little because we knew she meant what she said. Any new man in Sahnai's life was not getting a stamp of approval from baby sis.

"Inaya, I bought a house today for me and the boys because I am going to have my mom come up and help out until Sahnai is doing a hundred percent better. I know you got a lot going on, but I was wondering if you can swing by and grab the Black Card and just throw some beds and toilet paper in there. Some basic shit so my mom won't suffer. You are good at that kind of stuff, and I would rather be in the streets looking for Kadia than playing Martha Stewart." I finished my statement, hoping she would take pity on me.

"All right, Lox, I got you. I don't want my nephew sleeping on a hardwood floor or something crazy. Knowing you, the living room would have a futon instead of a couch. I'ma need the Black Card to be ready. I am on my way. Just text me the address so I can just throw it in the GPS quick. I already have some ideas for the boys' room."

I knew when I walked in this bitch tomorrow or the day after, it was going to look like some shit out of an interior design book. Inaya was bad ass when it came to that stuff. I still remembered the first time I stepped foot into her crib. I was blown away, especially considering that she did that shit without a Black Card or a stack of money. She made her house look like the front of a magazine on a tight-ass budget.

Deciding now would be the best time to call my mom and see if she would come up to help me, I dialed her next.

"Hello." My mother's sweet voice traveled through the phone. After talking about Sahnai and how she was doing and me asking about my pops, I asked moms to come up here and help me out.

"Mom, I really need you to come and help with the kids. I know you had no idea you had grandkids. Well, I still think you knew about li'l Q, but you didn't know about Aiden, and maybe you would enjoy spending time with them." I tried to make it sound sweet even though those two boys were a handful.

"Son, of course I do not mind. I may just stay down there so I can be around the boys and watch them grow. I thought Dana would have been helping you since she came down, but that girl lately, I tell you, Lennox. I do not know what is going on with her. Has she talked to you any?"

"Ma, what are you talking about? Dana is where? Here? I have not spoken to her since I was up there for Easter. She has not come by the house or called me. What is wrong with her little ass now?" I roared into the phone.

"Lennox Qualyl Hall, don't you yell at me. I have no idea what Dana's problem is. She won't talk to me, and I thought since she asked to come down there with you, she was there. She came down there three weeks ago. I will book a flight to come down tomorrow evening. I have some things to take care of before I leave. You try to find your sister and take care of all the drama you and Jahdair have caused. I know Sahnai is hurt because of some girl you were fucking. I am not stupid one bit. And what is this I hear about a missing child, Jahdair's girlfriend's kid? I wish you and your cousin would do better. The two of you are going to give me a gray hair." My mom fussed on and on for about half an hour before she finally said she had to go, like I was holding her up or something.

Sighing to myself, I realized I had one more call to make now, and that was to my little sister to try and find her. I understood that Dana's attitude and behavior was partially my and Phantom's fault. Shit, my dad too. She was his only daughter, and we all treated her like a queen since she was the baby of all of us. Even Azia spoiled her when we were growing up. We never told her no, and now she expected to always get her way. Getting her irritating-ass voicemail, I left her a short message.

"Yo, Dana, what the fuck, man? You in the Roc and never called me. Now Ma is worried. Call me back now. As a matter of fact, take your ass to the house. You got some explaining to do."

It is like the bullshit wouldn't end, one thing after another. Last night I caught this nigga Lamont straight talking shit about me and Phantom and how he had been robbing us on the low, but we were too stupid to catch on. He was in a bar, drunk, just flapping his gums when I got the call. I made my way to Déjà vu Lounge and snatched him up as soon as he stumbled out. I threw him in the trunk and drove to High Falls. I was not in the mood to shoot or dispose of a body, so I hit his head on the railing and pushed him over. He was drunk, so they would think he fell over and killed himself. Either way, I didn't have time for a whole torture, kill, and bury scenario. *Fuck him. His ass is swimming with the chemical-infused fishes now.*

Chapter 26

Inaya

Waking up to a wet pillow and the TV playing the talk shows, I felt beside me and realized that neither Kadia nor Phantom was there. I dreamed that Kadia was crying out to me in pain. *I can't take this anymore. I have to do something, figure out how to fix this. Even though it is Phantom's fault, it is mine too. I trusted him. I picked Noah's crazy ass to lie down with and have a child with. Everything that happened is crashing down on me. This is real. The man I fell in love with betrayed me, and my daughter is gone.* I kept checking my phone, hoping crazy-ass Noah would call or text. Eventually he would, because he just took my baby to get to me. It had nothing to do with Kadia at all. He didn't want to be a father or spend time with her. He really didn't have a huge interest in beating or hurting her unless he knew it hurt me. I used to pretend I didn't like my own daughter in front of him so he would stop grabbing her roughly by the arm or pinching her tiny legs.

I still remembered the first time I saw the black and blue bruises spread all over my baby's legs. I couldn't figure out what had happened to her. I checked the house for bugs or mice or loose objects that could have injured her since she had just began walking around. I had never seen any, but I was at a loss for what was causing my baby harm. Finally, I asked Noah, and he laughed at my panic and told me in a calm voice that he was disciplining her. I had no idea he was crazy until that moment. I picked up Kadia in one arm, holding her tight, and with my other hand I slapped him so hard in the face his eye began to bleed. That was when he turned around and kicked me in my ribs. Me and Kadia flew against the stove, where I hit my arm and it began to bleed.

I still remembered lying there, wondering what I had gotten myself into. I couldn't breathe for almost an hour, and I was just lying there moaning in pain and trying to get it together to stop my baby from screaming. I didn't know if she was hurt or if maybe something was broken or bleeding. I did protect her head with my arm so at least I knew her head was okay. I knew a baby's head was their most sensitive place on their body.

That was when I knew we had to leave someway somehow. I was young when I met Noah. I was 13 and he was 18 when we met. I was this skinny ugly duckling. I am not ashamed to admit it at all. I used to wear whatever clothes I could fit in once Sahnai didn't want them anymore. I had acne and frizzy hair. I had just gone back to live with my mom, who I had not lived with since I was 6 years old, and that was only because my grandma was getting sick. I would have been better off just staying with Sahnai and my grandma, because nothing had changed with my mother. She still treated me like I didn't matter at all. I was home alone all the time, having to figure out what to eat, having to figure out my homework on my own. I was raising myself.

Noah drove up next to me one day when I was walking home from school and asked me why a pretty girl like me was walking all alone. I laughed at him so hard I almost peed my pants. After I was done laughing, I told him he was too old for me, and I sadly watched him drive away.

That was the only time I could remember anyone but my grandmother telling me I was pretty. I didn't see Noah again for a few weeks, but then he came around again, parking his car and walking me home from school. He would bring me food from this chicken place, Country Sweet, or McDonald's. I was so busy looking for someone to love me back then that I was not able to see the monster behind the smiling face and empty compliments.

Once I ended up pregnant at 15, my mom told me I had to get out with my baby because she barely wanted to take care of me and sure as hell didn't want to take care of my baby too. That was when Noah suggested we come stay in Canada with him because he had a place there and that was where he usually lived. I had no idea I was supposed to get permission to go live there. Kadia and I went over with our birth certificates, and Noah told them I was his little sister going for a visit to his house. When I asked why, he assured me it was only because of my age and the fact that he didn't want to go to jail for having sex with a minor. So I went with it.

When Kadia was 2, I finally found a way to get away from him. It had been a whole year since I found out that Noah liked to beat on babies and women, and I was determined to find a way out. I used my cell phone to figure out what Greyhound bus would take me from downtown Toronto to Rochester and for how much. That was when I decided to take the money. I really didn't want to touch Noah's money, but he left me no choice. If I had to steal his dope money to save my daughter, then it was what it was. Just like a dumb nigga, he used to put his money in a Jordan shoebox that he stashed in his bottom dresser drawer. One day when he told me he would be gone for a few days, I decided it was now or never. Every few weeks he would be gone for about four days at a time. I honestly felt like he had another woman somewhere, but I was so happy when he was gone, I didn't give a fuck.

I fucked him good the day he left. I bust it open like never before and made sure to make him his favorite breakfast: French toast and eggs with fruit on the side. I waited a full day in case he decided to come back and saw that Kadia and I were gone. After he was gone for one day, I went into one of his black and gray Jordan shoeboxes and grabbed five stacks of money. I didn't take all of it. Shit, he still had another shoebox filled with hundreds. I wasn't trying to fuck him over. I was just trying to get my baby and me somewhere safe. Once we made our way to the bus station, I never looked back.

I guessed Noah knew I was thinking about him, because I got a text from an unknown number.

Unknown: If you want your daughter back, meet me at Genesee Park by the beginning to the wood trail. Don't come with anyone, or I will hurt her, and I want my money, bitch. Be there in two hours.

Me: Okay.

I didn't have the $18,000 I took from him. I guessed I could just bring him what I had and try to convince him to let Kadia and me go until I could get the rest of the money together. *Maybe I should call Phantom and ask him for the money. I should call him anyway and tell him what's up. I know he doesn't care about me, but he would want to help get Kadia home safe.*

Picking up the phone and scrolling to my favorites, I went to Phantom's name. Before I could click on the name, my phone rang in my hand, startling me. I almost dropped the damn thing. Seeing it was Cudjie, I decided to answer. *Maybe he can help me get the money to get Kadia back.*

"Hello," I answered in a low voice. My throat hurt from crying so much.

"Hey, ma, why you sound like that? You all right?"

"Hey, Cudjie, not really. Your boss Phantom gave my daughter to her father. Now he is holding her for ransom until I give him thousands of dollars," I cried.

"That's fucked up, shawty. I could have told you Phantom ain't no good. He hates women and kids. How he even know your baby father to begin with?"

Shit that is a good-ass question. How does Phantom know Noah? I been so busy worrying about my baby girl and my unborn baby that I didn't even pay attention to the details.

"Damn, I don't know how he knows Noah. Maybe their paths crossed in business."

"Did you say Noah? Nah, that is his boy from a long time ago. Shit, I didn't know he was Kadia's dad. I hate to break it to you, but I bet that is why he fucked wit' you. It was a setup, ma. I knew something was up, because that nigga Phantom hate kids, and him and Noah been hanging tighter than normal these last few months. Rumor has it that nigga Phantom even killed one of his shorties once because she wouldn't stop crying."

"I gotta go," I said, hanging up without waiting for a response. *What have I done? Why would I allow Kadia around another monster? What is wrong with me? Am I so desperate to be loved that I will allow anything to happen to my child? Maybe Kadia is better off without me anyway.* Seeing the knife next to the bed, I grabbed it and cut deep into the side of my arm, stopping before I could get to the vein. The picture of Kadia on her third birthday was sitting next to my bed. She had on her school uniform and a princess crown. She was smiling so big I could see her little teeth, and her hand was up in the air holding a bunch of pink and purple balloons. Some had hearts and cupcakes on them. I still remembered that day. I surprised her at school with cupcakes and balloons.

What was I thinking? I can't give up until I find my baby. Even though Sahnai is hurt and cannot be my support like she normally is, and Phantom is the enemy, I won't give up. Even if I am all alone. I will have to do this on my own. I will figure out a way to save us. I did it once before with no one's help. I can do it again. Throwing the knife down, I ran to my dresser and dug through the shirts, leaving a lot of them on the floor, and I grabbed my black lock box. Pushing in the random four numbers I used for everything private, I opened it up and grabbed the money I had been saving the past few months. Phantom was generous, and I barely spent it on what I didn't need, so I had a little over $5,000 saved. *I am giving this to Noah until I can get the rest of his money.* Looking at the picture I carried of Phantom, Kadia, and me one last time, I threw it in my lock box and ran down the stairs and out the front door.

Chapter 27

Phantom

Looking at the blood run down my hand and stain the sink, I was mad I could still see my reflection in the mirror. I was so disgusted at everything right now: this situation, the people who caused me to always think badly about every woman in my life. I had always been the kind of nigga who just did shit and didn't give a fuck. I was a boss, but this right here, what had I done? I lost the two most important people in my world. *The woman I love is never going to fuck with me again, and the little girl I love, shit, I can't even think about that. Naw, my li'l mama is coming home. I have every nigga I know in this little janky-ass city looking for Noah's bitch ass, and as soon as they find him, he is all mine.*

I picked up the phone and tried to call Iny for the hundredth time, but again, all I got was her voicemail and then an automated machine telling me the voicemail was full. I wished it were just me she was ignoring, but it wasn't. She wouldn't answer for anyone, and I had not seen her in days. Now that I thought about it, I had been trying to give her space so she could come to me in her own time. I knew she was hurt and mad and scared—hell, we were all scared for Kadia—but I also knew she loved me, and love is stronger than anything. At least, that's what people say. *Fuck it.* I had made a copy of Iny's key a while ago when I picked up Kadia for her because she had a late class. I was about to go over there and make her talk to me. *Maybe if I tell her I love her instead of just show her, we can work together to find baby girl.*

As soon as I walked in, I knew something was off, because the trash smelled awful and Inaya was a neat freak. Grabbing the trash and putting it on the back patio for now, I crept up the stairs.

"Iny," I called out quietly, but there was no answer. The house looked untouched, there was dust on the railing going upstairs, and all the lights were off. Where the hell could she be? Her old car was still parked in the lot, and I had the keys to the truck I bought her. She never came to pick them up. "Inaya," I called louder, making my way to her room.

Her bed was unmade, and Kadia's stuffed bear I bought her was in the bed. Next to the bed was what looked like drops of dried blood, and on her all-white comforter was a pool of dried blood. *What the hell?* Following them to the side of the bed, I found a knife next to the trash can. In the trash can was a purple box. *Wait, this shit says it's a pregnancy test.* Dumping the trash out, I found two tests with positive signs on them. *Iny is pregnant and she didn't tell me? Why is there a bloody knife? I know she would not kill herself when we don't know where Kadia is. Inaya has been through too much. She is not a weak female.*

Tearing the house up from top to bottom, I could not find a trace of her, and she left her car and purse behind. Her wallet was in the Louie bag, the one she bought when I gave her money to go shopping. Inside was her license and bank card. The only things missing were the picture of Kadia, her, and me that we took at the amusement park last month, and her phone. *This feels all wrong. My girl can't be hurt or dead. I can't lose anyone else I love.*

I can't lose her or my kids. My stomach was bubbling, and I felt like I was going to pass out. As I picked up the phone to call Lox, it began to ring in my hand. Not recognizing the number that was a code with four numbers then a dash and two more numbers, I picked up.

"Hello," I answered.

"Phantom," cried a tiny voice.

"Kadia, is that you? Hello, Kadia, where are you?" I yelled into the phone.

Hearing the dial tone in my ear, I couldn't wrap my mind around this shit. Too much was going on. I needed Kadia back home, and now I couldn't find Iny. *Like, why this nigga Noah playing wit' me? I'ma catch up to him soon, and when I do, I am not even going to hesitate to do what I have to do.* I met Noah by accident one day when Kadia and I were at the movies. He came up to me with tears in his eyes asking how I knew his daughter and giving me a sob story about how her mother kidnapped her from his house a year ago and he had not seen her since. I took the nigga's number but really wasn't going to let him around Kadia until I spoke to Iny, but one day, I overheard her say how she would never allow Noah in Kadia's life. Then all that shit happened with Lox not knowing he had a kid, and I started to feel like letting Noah in Kadia's life was something I needed to do.

I let my bullshit and Lox's bullshit endanger my baby girl, and now my girl and baby were missing. All this shit because I was too busy not wanting to trust Iny and believing that she was like everybody else. I was about to get serious in these streets. I killed a few people who said they did business with this nigga. His name was Noah, but the streets called him Kwame. I found out he was a low-level hustler who sneaked weed across the border into Canada.

Reaching for my phone, I started with this nigga I knew named Sin, in Buffalo. This dude knew everyone who be moving shit across the border. Putting it on speaker while it rang, I started to clean up the house. I didn't want my girls coming home to no messy, stinking house. I knew that would really get to Iny, and she didn't need to be stressing and doing all those extra movements while she was pregnant with my seed.

"Yo, nigga, what's good?" he finally answered.

"Yo, I need some info on a nigga named Noah, goes by the name of Kwame. Normally I wouldn't even ask, but the nigga kidnapped my little girl, and I gotta get her back."

"Damn, I know that nigga. He is strange as fuck, too. I swore he was dating an old-ass bitch once, seen him hugging and kissing her in the Galleria Mall, but when I asked him who he was wit', he said that's his moms. I'ma text you his number and an address where I know him and his people handle business in the Roc. Man, good luck on finding your little one. I would fucking go crazy if someone snatched one of mine. Holla if you need us to come down there. You know me and Donavan gotcho back, and crazy-ass Savage up here, too. Yo, for real, fam, find your little girl, and when you do, keep her close to you. When my baby moms got killed the other day because of my ex, that shit killed me. I wasn't even paying attention. I didn't fight for her at all."

"Thanks, man. This shit is stressful, and honestly, I caused this to happen. I'ma hit you later and update you. Good looking out, nigga. One."

Seeing the number come through, I decided not to call right away. First, I was going to that nigga's trap to sit on that bitch until he came through or he forced me to make examples out of his people.

Pulling up to the spot Sin told me about on this little dead-end street called Judson Terrace, I could tell exactly what house he was using as a trap. The two-toned brown house looked like it was falling apart, kind of leaning to the left, and two young niggas were sitting outside on some chairs smoking and laughing. Not a care in the world for those two, but I bet all of that shit was about to change fast. Not wanting to bother Lox because he had enough on his plate, I texted one of the little niggas named Tae. He was a kid we took off the streets and showed how to make money, and he was loyal as fuck for it, too. He basically be running our traps, watching the snakes, and making sure the money is right. Especially now with all these distractions Lox and I had going on.

An hour later and no one but these two jokers and a few junkies came or went in the spot. Out of the corner of my eye, I saw Tae walking slowly through the cut and making his way to my all-black Ford pickup.

"Hey, little nigga, good looking on getting here so fast. You got that wit' you?"

"Hell, yeah, I got two of them thangs," he responded, lifting up his black hoodie and showing me two chrome nines.

"Good looking, son. As soon as it gets dark, we going in. I can't waste no more time on this shit. My little girl been gone long enough, and now my shorty is missing too. This nigga Noah thinks he a slick one, but I got something for that ass." Tae just hit me with a head nod and leaned back to watch the scene.

I picked up my phone and went to my pictures. All ten pictures in there were of Iny and Kades. Shit, I'd never been the kind of nigga who had pictures of anyone in my phone. Honestly, I didn't even know how to work the camera, but Kadia loved taking pictures. The last picture I had never seen before, but I realized it was from the day I let Noah take her. She was making some silly face with her eyes scrunched up and her tongue sticking out. She had on her little blue jean overalls with a white shirt. I could see her little Pandora bracelet I got her shining from the sun behind her.

I can't let my feelings distract me right now. Going to contacts, I clicked on Iny's name and hit connect. This time it didn't even ring. It went right to voicemail. Banging my fists on the steering wheel, I startled Tae, who looked at me with questioning eyes.

"Yo, let's go do this shit. I am tired of waiting, and it's dark enough now." Yanking my hood over my head and throwing some shades on, I grabbed the extra nine and made sure I had my other Glock in my hand and ready to go. We quietly made our way to the house. I signaled to Tae for him to go through the front and I would take the back.

Chapter 28

Inaya

Running out of the house, I decided to call a taxi to meet me around the corner at the gas station, because I did not want Phantom to know I was going to meet Noah. *I don't want this nigga to step in and do what he thinks is right or help Noah fuck me up so I never see Kadia again.* I kept thinking about what Cudjie said about Noah being friends with Phantom. At first I felt crushed. Why would he intentionally do that to Kadia, to me? But the more I thought about it, the more it didn't make sense. If Phantom and Noah were friends, why did I never see Noah come here or call Phantom's phone? Plus, Lox never mentioned anyone named Noah. I mean, I understood him wanting to hurt me because Phantom didn't give a fuck about me, but I knew the love he had for my daughter was real. Plus, I remembered Lox telling me that Cudjie was not anyone I should be involved with, so that meant he was most likely not very trustworthy.

Looking back at Phantom's window one last time, I ignored the bad feeling in the pit of my stomach and walked quickly to the Sunoco on the corner. Seeing the yellow cab pull up, I slid in and told him my destination. Running my hand across the worn leather in the cab as we pulled off and headed down Elmwood, I couldn't help but think this could be it. Noah could kill me or do anything to me, but all I needed to make sure of was that Kadia made it out okay. I wanted to call Phantom, but I left my phone home in my bedside drawer. I turned it off because I knew the first thing he would try was to GPS my phone if he noticed I was missing, if he cared that I was missing.

Sadly, there was a part of me that still wished Phantom would love me. I wanted him to be my Prince Charming or knight in shining armor, the one who rolled up on a white horse and slayed my enemies, the one to protect me forever and love me forever.

"How much?" I asked the driver as he pulled in by the pool.

"Eighteen even," he replied.

Handing him a $20 bill and grabbing the Old Navy tote I had the money in, I slowly walked down the path. As soon as I got to the beginning of the running trail at the edge of the woods, I could see Noah's figure. Looking at him up close, I saw he had not changed much. He was still rocking his hair in tight curls on the top of his head, and he didn't look like he'd gained any weight. I could see his muscles straining against his light blue Diesel shirt. He had on khaki cargo shorts and some low-top white-on-white Uptowns. His Ray-Ban shades were covering his eyes, so I couldn't guess his mood, but the smirk on his face told me what I needed to know.

"Let's go." He roughly pushed me in the direction of his red Honda. Once he started it up, he had the nerve to turn the music up and start rapping to some Rick Ross song, bobbing his head like I was not here to get my daughter, who he kidnapped. My anger bubbled to the surface, and I turned that music right the fuck down.

"I didn't come here to go on a cruise around town. I want my daughter. Where is Kadia? Why didn't you bring her with you?" I knew he could see how upset I was by the look on my face. I was trying to keep my cool and not cry and give him an opening to start playing more games with me.

"She is not with me right now as you can see. Don't touch my fucking music again." That was all he said before he turned up the music and kept driving. After we drove for about an hour, I noticed we were headed away from Rochester toward Syracuse, but instead of us riding on the I-90, we were flying down these bumpy-ass back roads. I kept praying the deer I saw grazing at the side of the road didn't decide to jump out in front of us and cause a crash before I could get to my baby. I knew yelling at and fighting Noah was not going to get me anywhere, especially since I was on the expressway. So I decided to just chill until he took me to Kadia.

After a while he stopped at an apartment building on a deserted street and jumped out of the car. He began talking to a man with a red polo shirt and nappy hair. Looking around to see if Kadia was there, I didn't see her come out. After a few more minutes passed, the red-shirt guy passed Noah something in a brown bag, and he hopped back in the car and began driving again. I thought about asking him where Kadia was again but then decided I should keep quiet and see where we ended up next.

We pulled up to a house on Cuba Place in the hood. I wondered if he was making another run to pick up some drugs or something. *I know he is a horrible father, but would he really be keeping her in this place?* The house looked like it was being eaten from the inside out by rats or some other vermin. Slowly following Noah after he opened my door, I immediately wanted to throw up once he opened the front door and we stepped in. I swallowed that shit though and started breathing through my mouth, trying to keep the smell out of my nose. *I don't*

want this sick motherfucker knowing I am pregnant. I
have to protect this baby too.

"Kadia," I called out, not seeing her anywhere. I didn't
see any toys or kids' clothes. *Where is she?* Looking
around on my own while Noah played on his phone, the
more I saw, the more worried I got. Running up the stairs
and looking in each room, I didn't see any sign of Kadia.
What the fuck is going on? I couldn't help but wonder
if he and Phantom were playing a game with my mind.
Maybe he never had Kadia and Phantom lied. I ran back
into the front room. I guessed it was a living room if you
could call it that. There was one old box TV sitting on a
milk crate and a couch that looked like it had seen better
days. Seeing Noah laughing, I knew coming here was a
mistake.

"Oh, Inaya Marie, you never changed. You're still
stupid when it comes to that little brat of yours. Anyway,
let's get to the most important things. First of all, you
look good. Growing up really filled you out in all the
right places. I guess you been drinking your milk. I can't
wait to find out how that grown-up pussy feels." As he
gave me this little speech, he began grabbing my breast
through my Nike Pro shirt. Really, what an idiot. Did he
think I would willingly give him this pussy? Slapping his
hands away, I tried to get him to focus on the reason I
was here: our daughter.

"Noah, again, I am only here for Kadia. I came to get
her and bring her back home. Now please bring her out of
wherever you are hiding her so I can leave."

"Leave? Ha-ha! You are mine now. Second thing, Inaya,
where is my fucking money? Oh, bitch, did you think I
forgot? Naw, now run my shit so we can move on to me
feeling on that body."

I handed him the colorful Old Navy bag I was holding
with the $5,000 in it. He quickly snatched it from my

hand and shoved me on the dirty-ass couch. He started counting the money with a deep frown on his face while once again I found myself trying not to get sick. *This baby is making being here a lot harder than I originally thought it would be.*

"Noah, look, I know it's only five thousand right now. That's all I have. I will get you the rest. I have a new truck I can sell and will have the other fifteen in a week or so. I didn't have time to sell it before I got here. If you need it sooner, I have someone I can ask. Now can you please grab Kadia so we can go?" I asked as I stood up and tried to make my way toward the door.

"Inaya, you don't get it, do you? I got rid of Kadia, and honestly I don't give a fuck about this money," he stated as he threw the bag to the floor. "I wanted you, and I used Kadia to get you here. Now you are mine, and you are going to make up for all the time you have been away and for touching my money."

Hearing him say Kadia was gone made me drop to my knees on the dirty hardwood floors. Not being able to hold it in anymore, I started to throw up while shaking and crying at the same time.

"You killed our daughter? You are sick! What a monster you are!" I screamed.

Chapter 29

Phantom

As soon as I hit the back door at this nigga Noah's trap, I didn't waste any time trying to sneak around and be quiet. Honestly, I didn't even give a fuck anymore. I picked up my size-ten Timberland boot and kicked the flimsy wooden door right out of the frame. As soon as I made that move, I ran into the living room to see the same two little niggas jump up off the couches, one reaching for a little-ass pistol. Tae grabbed one and I grabbed the other. I shot him in the head before I said a word. His little sidekick pissed himself and began crying, telling us the money was stashed in the ceiling panel in the kitchen.

"Little nigga, I didn't come for no money or drugs. I got my own money. Where that nigga Noah at?" I asked with authority in my voice.

"I really don't know, man. I don't really see him. His man Chink always come and give us the re-up and collect the money," he stuttered.

"Tae, hold this nigga while I search this motherfucker." I checked the house from top to bottom, and no one else was there. All I found was a scrap of paper with some bitch's number on it. Snatching that off the dresser in the upstairs room, I ran down the stairs, shooting the kid in his leg and shoulder. I threw his cell phone to him. "Tell

Noah I am looking for his ass and I want back what he took from me *now*."

Me and Tae calmly walked out the front door and into the night like nothing ever happened. After I got in my truck, I pulled out and decided to stop somewhere and get some grub. I turned onto Genesee and decided to go to This Is It and grab a jerk chicken meal. Seeing Ashena, my little jump off who worked at the gas company, call me, I decided to answer. *Inaya not fucking with me, and I need to release some of this stress.*

"Yo."

"Hey, Phantom, what you doing? I want to see you. Remember you owe me for that favor the other day."

"All right. You remember the crib you came to last time out in Brighton? Come check me out there. I am on my way now." Not giving her a chance to keep talking in my ear, I hung up as soon as she confirmed she knew the place. Lox and the boys were at their new house, and it was just me in the townhouse alone now. I really didn't like to bring any random chicks home, but I was tired of being in this bitch alone.

Pulling up to the parking lot and parking next to Inaya's truck, I couldn't help but wonder where she was for the hundredth time today. I hate the fact that I couldn't get her off my mind. She was a distraction I really didn't need right now.

Seeing Ashena walk up to the door, I opened it before she had a chance to knock.

"Hey, babe, I am glad you finally came around and called me. I know you been checking for me for a while now. I figured you just got busy or something." I could see her talkative, nosy ass looking all over the living room. Since Inaya did not decorate my place, it was not showroom quality, but it was not too bad since Azia actually came and picked all the furniture for us. She told me she wanted to be comfortable when she came for a visit.

Waiting, I guessed for her ass to be finished so we could head to the bedroom, she instead walked on my cream carpet into the living room with her shoes on and plopped her ass on my couch, making herself comfortable. Seeing my frown, she got the hint and took her shoes off, walking them back to the front area where I had a wooden shoe rack.

"Phantom, why do you have all of these little girl shoes and sandals at the front door? Does your cousin have kids?"

"Damn, you nosy as fuck. Yeah, my cousin has kids, two boys. Since I can see you not 'bout to leave this shit alone, the shoes belong to my daughter. Any other questions I can answer for you?"

"Sorry. As long as we been messing around, I never knew you had kids."

I didn't even bother to respond. I just grabbed her hand and led her upstairs to my bedroom. "Make yourself comfortable. I'ma go shower and I will be back." I made sure to turn the TV on and hand her the remote before I made my way to the bathroom. Turning the water on hot, I stripped out of my clothes and grabbed a clean rag out of the linen closet. Stepping in and closing my eyes, I leaned my head against the tile and let the water beat down over my back and neck.

God, I know me and you don't talk much. I really need you right now. I know you have always watched over me and Azia, and for that I thank you. I want . . . no, I need you to help me, Lord. I messed up and I am sorry. Please bring Kadia home safely and let Inaya be okay. I promise when she makes it home, I will spend the rest of my life showing her how much I love her. Amen.

Hearing the bathroom door click, I knew exactly what was up. *I guess Ashena is not worried about her hair, because she must want to get fucked in this shower. If she steps in, that's it. I ain't worried about no hairstyle. This ain't lovemaking.* Shorty stepped in the water with a black lace bra and panty set. Her brown hair curled up as soon as it got wet, and her skin was glistening in the water. Dropping to her knees, she took my man in her mouth and began teasing the head with her tongue. *Damn, this shit feels good.* Feeling my dick slide to the back of her mouth, I couldn't help but let out a moan. Seeing shorty play with her pink pussy while she was sucking my dick made me feel like I was going to nut in her mouth right now. She took her finger from her pussy to her lips and began licking off her own cum.

Fuck! I can't take this shit no more. If I don't fuck it now, I'ma cum all over her face. Grabbing her by her hair, I roughly turned her over and moved those panties to the side, not caring if I ripped them. Shoving my dick in her tight-ass pussy, I stood there and watched her fat ass bounce as she worked the shit out of my cock. Feeling my nut on its way, I grabbed her right leg and went to work.

"Phantom, stop. It hurts. Be gentle, baby." She was screaming, but I wasn't paying no fucking attention. I felt like a dog in heat, and I couldn't stop even if I wanted to. As soon as I was done busting all over her back, I smacked her ass one good time and got out. Sliding on some boxers, basketball shorts, and a wife-beater, I lay back on my bed drifting in and out of sleep. *I guess that fuck was what I needed.*

I woke up in the middle of the night to Kadia crying. Looking around and realizing the person next to me was not Inaya, I slowly figured out it must have been a dream. Shoving Ashena off of me, I got up to go piss, and that was when I heard it again. There was definitely someone crying. Running downstairs after grabbing my gun, I flung open the door only to see something wrapped in some silk sheet or something lying in a heap in front of my door. It took me a minute before I realized what was happening, but as soon as I spotted Kadia's little pink socks with white hearts all over sticking out, I snatched the bundle up and moved the silky fabric from her face. *Oh, my God, it's Kadia.*

"Daddy Phantom, it hurts so bad," she cried out.

Running in the house with her, I ran upstairs and set her on her bed. Totally unwrapping her tiny body, what I saw brought tears to my eyes. For once in my life I was not ashamed of crying in front of anyone, or in general. Kadia had welts all over her body and red chafing. Her knees were bleeding, as was her face, and all she had on were a pair of white panties and her socks. *What the fuck?* All I could see was red because I wanted to kill Noah with my bare hands, nice and slow.

Kadia's cries brought me back to the here and now. Not really knowing what to do, I just held her and kept telling her I was sorry and she was safe now. Knowing I had to take her to the hospital, I went in her closet and grabbed a sweat suit and a clean blanket. I stripped the black silk robe completely off. I kept thinking it looked familiar, and it smelled like cheap perfume and incense. Getting that dirty stuff off of her and putting clean clothes on her, I picked her up and wrapped her in the blanket. I went to run down the stairs until Ashena wandered into my view. *Fuck.* I forgot all about her ass.

"Phantom, who is that? Is that your little girl?" she asked while reaching out her hand like she wanted to touch Kades.

Snatching Kades away, I thought to myself, *here we go with fucking twenty questions.* "Yo, ma, put your stuff on now. I gotta take my baby to the hospital, and I don't have time for the great inquisition. You not my girl or my baby moms, so back the fuck off and don't ever reach for my kid again. She ain't no puppy for randoms to be stroking her and shit."

Lucky for her, she turned and got dressed fast and took the hint and made her way to the front door. Not giving a fuck about her attitude or little mad face, I followed directly behind her and got baby girl in the car. As soon as I had her settled, I called her great-grandmother to meet us at the hospital. I hated to worry her, but I couldn't find Inaya, and Sahnai was in the hospital. Someone had to be with me who had a legal say over Kadia. Luckily Lox was over there with the kids, so he was going to bring her to the hospital.

Speeding as fast as I dared with Kades in the back, we made it to Strong Hospital in no time. I didn't even waste any time trying to park. I threw my keys at the valet and rushed baby girl inside, praying that her injuries were only what I could see and not something more.

Chapter 30

Sahnai

Waking up, I began to wonder where I was, and then I remembered being stabbed and hearing Lox talking to me for what seemed like a long time. He told me how sorry he was and that he was never leaving me again. *Well, shit, for someone who is never leaving me again, where the fuck he at right now? I want him to hurry up and appear so I can see my son. I need to know he is okay and hold him in my arms.*

I buzzed the nurse a few minutes later, and a pleasant older black lady walked in and began removing the tubes from my mouth and nose.

"Hey, baby, we are so happy you finally came around and woke up. You have a lovely family. That husband of yours, ooh, boy, if I were young, I would have been trying to get at him myself. They were up here all the time, day and night. Your sister crying all over you, praying, and begging you to wake up. Just lovely they were, all except that mean-looking one with the black eyes. I bet he can fuck, but his manners are just missing all the way around." I swore these nurses were bold nowadays, but instead of being offended by her unprofessionalism, I found it funny.

Laughing, I knew right away she was talking about Phantom's mean ass. He was mean even when Lox and

I used to date back in the day. I didn't know how the hell he and my cousin agreed. She must have liked his craziness, but me, I was all good on shit like that.

Looking around the room, I didn't find my cell phone or my handbag, but I was sure Inaya had my stuff somewhere safe. On the bedside table were red roses, my favorite, and little coloring papers that I assumed Q and Kadia made for me. I missed my baby cousin too, and baby Aiden. I loved him like he was mine, and I hoped Lox and I could make this thing work out. I wanted my family to be together, and I wanted to make it up to him, all the bullshit I put him through by running away and not telling him about Q.

Asking the nurse if I could take a shower since I felt gross, she told me to take a sponge bath for now until they could come and check my wounds to make sure I was healed enough. Looking down at myself for the first time, I noticed the bulkiness from the thick bandages under my Victoria's Secret nightshirt. Damn, to think I came that close to losing my life, over what? I guessed over Lox, not that he wasn't worth it, but to almost die because he was fucking nasty-ass Toya? That was crazy. I hoped he handled her before I did. He claimed he loved me so much, but I didn't remember any talk when I was in a coma of him taking care of that bitch and getting rid of her. I didn't care if she was pregnant with Phantom's baby. Shit, he said it wasn't his anyway, so fuck it.

Slowly easing off the bed to make my way to the bathroom, I had to keep stopping and holding on to my IV pole because the pain was unbearable. By the time I made it across the tiny room and to the bathroom, I had to sit on the toilet to catch my breath. I wondered how long I would be like this, weak as a newborn kitten and in more pain than anytime I had ever remembered.

Seeing a Pink duffel bag and a Pink travel bag with soap, deodorant, a brush, and extra clothes, I knew Inaya had been up here taking care of business. Looking at myself in the mirror, I could see she had my hair taken care of and my eyebrows done.

As I began slowly washing up with the Caress body wash and changing into a fresh nightshirt, I began thinking about all it looked like my cousin did for me. I really loved her. She always had my back. I loved this nightshirt she picked out for me. It was white with pink hearts and black letters saying, "Love." She also packed some matching pink Ralph Lauren booties for my feet. I hated to have my feet feel cold. Noticing my toes painted a light blue, I smiled to myself. The last time Inaya painted my toes was when I was sick as a kid. I was around 12 and she had just turned 10. I had to have my appendix taken out, and she stayed up under me when I came home from the hospital. I was on a lot of painkillers the first few days and was pretty out of it, so I slept a lot. I remembered waking up one day and looking at my toes. Inaya had painted them as a surprise to make me feel better, but at 10, she had nail polish on my toenails, toes, and the couch I was sleeping on.

Smiling at the memories, I opened the bathroom door and stopped short when I thought I heard Lox's voice in the hallway. Creeping over to the door of the room, I opened it to see him hugging that bitch Toya and saying something in her ear before handing her some money and turning around to walk toward my room. *Is this nigga kidding me? I am in a coma, and he is fucking the enemy? Giving this bitch money?* As soon as he noticed me, he had a huge smile and tried to come over and hug me.

"Naw, nigga, you good. Go hug Toya. Did you pay that tramp to stab me or what?"

"What? I was hugging her and thanking her for saving Kadia's life. Why don't you just sit down before you hurt yourself and calm down a bit. Come on," he said, trying to lead me back to the bed.

Snatching away from him and feeling my chest burn, I wished I had thought before I made that movement. I slowly climbed in the bed and gave him the dirtiest look, all the while rolling my eyes and trying not to cry out in pain.

"Look, Lox, just go get Q and bring him to me and get the fuck out. Inaya can keep him while I am in here. We don't need you for shit. I can't believe after all that bitch did, you are all in her face, especially in front of my hospital room door. You are brave, I am just gonna tell you that."

Before he could even think of a comeback to try to save himself, the door opened, and in walked the last person I expected to see. "Yo, ma, I am so happy you up. I been so worried about you. You left Maryland and said you would be gone a few weeks, and it's been a few months. What is up with that? And who is this nigga chillin' up in here wit' you?" Honest leaned down and kissed me, not waiting for me to say who Lox was, and then he sat his ass on my bed and grabbed my hand. Shit, I was not ever expecting to see him again.

"Honest, this is my baby father, Lox. I just woke up, babes, after being stabbed by his other baby moms, and I am just making arrangements with him to have my son brought to me and then to go home with my cousin instead of him since he is still sleeping with the enemy."

Looking at Lox's face, I could tell he was pissed. His eyes were almost gray, and his hands were clenched at his side like he wanted to slap the fuck out of me. *Well, let me throw some more fuel on the fire.*

"Lox, this is my fiancé from Maryland. Everyone calls him Honest." Now Honest and I were never even girl-friend or boyfriend, so no idea where I pulled that shit from, and I just added the part about us being engaged to piss Lox off and hurt him how he hurt me.

"Shorty, you are a piece of work. I wonder if your man would like to know who was fucking it just last week. Maybe you should tell him how I came in your mouth or how you was fucking me raw. As for Q, once you get rid of this lame-ass nigga, call me and you can visit with him. In case you're interested, Noah kidnapped Kadia. Toya, who is also his baby moms, saved her before Noah's mother killed the poor child. As for your cousin who came up here and took care of your ungrateful ass while she was worried and searching for her little girl, she is now missing. I don't know why you didn't turn out like Inaya." He just stared at me like I was going to jump to my knees and beg for forgiveness or some other lame shit.

"Fuck you, Lox. Now get out and don't come back until you have my son witchu," I yelled out. Watching him shake his head like he was sorry for me and walk out of the room, I couldn't help but feel a bit of sadness. He was the only man I ever loved, but I wouldn't allow him to hurt me, especially with the bitch who tried to kill me. Just that quick I felt like, *fuck Inaya, for real. Everyone always thinks she is so perfect and always telling me I should be more like her*. Yeah, her daughter was missing, and she came up here to be by my side. Woo-ha. She was fucking amazing, and just like when we were younger, I ain't shit.

Rolling on my side to look at the wall, I hoped that Honest would leave soon so I could sort things out in my mind and heart.

Chapter 31

Lox

This fucking girl, I tell you. Every day with her was something new. She didn't ask if Kadia was all right or worry about Inaya. Nope. She was too busy playing games. I had too much other shit going on in my life to be here chasing a female who didn't want to be caught. I knew one thing: my son wouldn't be going anywhere with her and her ol' monkey-looking-ass friend who came busting up in there like he was Captain Save-a-ho. I noticed when I spoke though that he shut the fuck up. His skin was all dark and light at the same time from using bleach, and his eyes were bloodshot from smoking too much weed. And his lips looked black, like he dipped them shits in tar.

Fuck it. That's what I get for trying to be a good nigga and settle down and shit. One thing I would always be was a good father though. My mom came in a few days ago and had been home with the kids. I finally found my sister Dana's ass, and she was acting as strange as ever. She was drunk when I found her ass in some club for 21 and older, no clue how she even got in. She was mumbling about why he would cheat, and she was so sad the whole way home, so I guessed some little boy broke her heart, but I need her to get up out of her feelings. Stopping to get some pizza and wings for me and the family so my mom didn't have to cook, I parked my white Audi and ran into Little Caesars. I didn't even have the patience to wait for some shit to be made, and this was the only spot I could think of where the food was ready to walk out the door.

I was back in the car and driving down Monroe Avenue in a few minutes. I was fucking happy that Sahnai was awake, not just because I loved and cared about her ass but because I could now focus on getting shit together in my life and spending time with my kids. First thing tomorrow I was going to check up on all of our spots and make sure money was right and that no one felt any kind of way about Lamar's sudden demise. He may have had a partner on the inside, so I had to feel these niggas out. Then I was hitting the mall up for my kids to buy them some shit.

Pulling into my driveway, I hopped out of the car carrying the food in one hand and my keys in the other. Once I got in and closed the door, I could hear my mom yelling at Dana. Shit, she was yelling so loud I knew she didn't hear me come in yet. Standing in the front hallway and listening to them in the kitchen, I couldn't believe what I was hearing.

"Dana, mind your business, little girl. What me and your father are going through is not your business at all. If I wanted to talk about my problems with my man, I would call a friend, not talk to a child who is smelling herself and is fast in my business. You hear me, little girl?"

"Oh, my father? Ha-ha, you are so funny, Mother. Are you sure he is my father? You think I don't notice how he avoids me and how he treats me? He is closer to Azia than me, and why is that? Is that why he is cheating on you, Mother? Because you cheated on him? What will you do when he leaves you for this girl in the States? I heard they have kids together. Right under your nose you allowed him to play you. You are no better than Phantom's mom. You are a hypocrite and a poor example for me," my sister verbally attacked my mom.

I didn't want to intervene yet, because I was waiting for my mother's response. *All this time my father has been cheating on her?* I mean, I knew he did when they were younger. He and I talked about this when I turned 16 and he gave me his man-to-man talk. He told me that even though he was away from my mom most of the time, he had outgrown all the different types of pussy and I should start out not cheating on the woman I decided to settle down with, the one I fell in love with the way he was in love with my mom.

Hearing a slap and then my mother's voice, I began to walk toward the kitchen but almost choked when I heard what she said next.

"No, Dana, he is your father. I am not a cheater no matter what you think. How could you not know he is your dad? You look just like him with those crazy-ass green eyes, and you even have his nose and ears. The reason your father is not close to you is because he thinks you're a lesbian. He says you behave mannish and look like you love women, and he is not going to accept that from his only daughter, so he tries to forget you exist!"

Well, I was not expecting to hear that. I guessed I never noticed my dad and Dana's relationship. Phantom and I were close to him, and I just assumed that him not being close to Dana was because she was a girl and still kind of a kid compared to the rest of us. *I have to make a point of calling my dad and ask him what the fuck is going on and get my mom alone and ask her what's up.* I wondered if this was why Dana was acting out so much. She even dropped out of college at the end of last term. My mom didn't know. She thought that Dana was just on summer vacation. I needed my pops to figure out his wife and kid, because I was done with all the drama. I loved my mom and my sister, but their problem was clearly not with me.

Opening the kitchen door, I could see Dana sitting at the table crying and my mom sitting across from her with an angry look on her face and her light skin turning beet red.

"Evening. Dana, what's wrong with you?"

"Leave me alone," she yelled at me and ran up the stairs.

"Little girl, remember this my damn house. Respect me," I screamed up the stairs. I wanted to go upstairs and grab her and fuck her up, but I was sure I would be going to jail. "Ma, any word from Phantom on Inaya yet?"

"No, they still cannot find her. I am praying every moment I have free. I do not like that she has been gone so long. I hope Phantom finds her soon. She is a good girl. I like her for him. She is better than Shawnie. That Shawnie was no good, pure evil."

"I know, Mom. After I nap for a while, I'ma go check him and see what he knows and what we can do. We will bring her home. You're right. Li'l sis is a good girl, and I know cuz gave her a real hard time at first. You know how he is. He can be a real asshole, and he was to her, but after a while he couldn't help it. She stole his heart."

"I didn't know he gave her a hard time. When he brought her and Kadia to visit, he was really sweet to her. Except when he introduced her, he said it was his friend. I was surprised because Kadia was calling him Daddy, but I minded my business and didn't say anything. When he gave her money to go shopping with Azia though, I knew she was special. You know how he is about spending his money on women." My mom laughed and so did I. Phantom was mean as hell with his money. He never even gave Shawnie a dime. When they had a kid, he paid all bills and bought anything that was needed.

"Ma, Sahnai woke up today, but since she is making some poor life choices, I am not letting her have li'l Q. I am going to keep him with me and Aiden. I don't want to talk about it right now either. I am beat, and I need to lie down." I could see my mom wanted to know details, but fuck that. A nigga had not slept in at least three days. My family thought I was a robot, but I liked rest too. Before taking care of kids and having one who cried a lot and one who wanted to play all the time, I had more time to just chill when I felt like it. Seeing my king-size bed with the fluffy white and navy blue comforter, I felt like someone gave me a gift. Shit, Inaya did a great job decorating my house. She called this comforter a hotel set. I guessed it was the same shit they used in the hotels or something. My only complaint was all these fucking pillows she got in the bed. I guessed she felt like she had to cover some of the space or something. I always ended up throwing them on the floor in my sleep.

Stripping down to my boxers and marina, I jumped in the bed and rolled onto my stomach. I didn't know why I liked to sleep like this. Maybe it was from my rape trauma. I was protecting my dick. I kind of wished I were lying next to Sahnai, or anyone. I mean, yeah, I was a nigga, but I got lonely too. I spent so long waiting to find another love like what I had with Sahnai, and then I found Sahnai, and things went all to hell. I began to drift in and out of sleep thinking about her touch, her pouty lips, and how they felt on my skin.

Waking up the next morning, I decided to stop at the hospital and check on Sahnai since she was on my mind when I went to sleep. But when I got there, the receptionist said she checked herself out early. *Well, fuck it. I guess it wasn't meant to be.* I was actually coming to apologize about the Toya thing and see if we could get back on track. *Maybe I will try to stop at the house later, or maybe this is a sign from God.*

Pulling up to Eastview Mall, I decided to hit up H&M first and get the boys some clothes. I remembered the first time I tried to buy them some clothes, it took Sahnai and Inaya to show me how to read these fucking sizes. I mean, shit, I had no idea what "months" and "T" and "yrs." all meant.

Seeing some cute little girl skirts and shit, I made sure to grab some shit for Kadia, too. I needed li'l mama to smile. When I saw her last night, she was so quiet and sad. She was a little girl who liked gifts and surprises, so I was sure this would do the trick. Not stopping until the little basket was full, I went to cash out and move on to the next store.

Finally walking out of Foot Locker with new Jordans for all three kids, I made one last stop at Pandora in the mall. Kadia cried because she lost the bracelet Phantom gave her when she was kidnapped, so I decided to get her a new one.

"Sir, can I help you?"

"Yes, I need a Pandora bracelet for a little girl with a few charms on it. I am not really sure what they are or what the difference is with all of the ones I see. Just give me the nicest one you got."

"This is the size bracelet for a small child. Let me know if you think this is the correct size. Here are some charms. What does the lucky little girl like to do?"

"Well, she likes soccer, toys, the colors purple, blue, and pink, and all kinds of dolls and other girl shit."

"We have initials, dolls, soccer balls, and more in this case all with pink and purple stones. Why don't you browse and let me know when you see something you like?"

Looking at all the little girly shit, I was truly lost. "Yo, ma, why don't you come back over here and just pick out enough charms to fill the bracelet."

She quickly set seven charms on the counter. I liked it. There were purple and pink spacers, a pink dress, a princess crown, a few hearts, and a Cinderella carriage. She matched them all up with colors and shit.

"Thanks. I will take them all, and the bracelet. Please put them in a gift box."

"Sir, these charms are almost ninety dollars apiece. Are you sure?"

"Yo, I never asked you about any price. Just wrap that up quick so I can get it to my niece," I told her with an attitude, throwing a bunch of $100 bills on the counter. I turned my back to her while she finished so I wouldn't cuss her ass out. Finally, she finished, and snatching my package and receipt, I walked away, ignoring her when she told me I overpaid.

"Yo, Phantom, I am on my way to come see Kadia. I bought her little spoiled ass some shit, too."

"Man, she gonna be another damn Azia and Dana, keep on. I will see you when you get here, my nigga." Phantom hung up, laughing.

I guessed he was right, but fuck it. She had two boy cousins, so she was supposed to be spoiled. Jumping in the Audi, I jumped on the 490 East, bumping my music and trying to let go of all the stress.

Chapter 32

Inaya

Feeling Noah grab me by the back of my hair and fling me to the ground, I immediately crunched in a ball to protect my unborn baby. I lay there for what seemed like an hour waiting for him to finish with a kick, or a few, to be exact. Suddenly I felt and saw at the same time a huge black ant crawling across my arm. Jumping up and screaming, I turned to see Noah sitting on the couch drinking a beer and laughing at me.

"Oh, Inaya, sweet little Inaya. Why don't you have a seat since you will be here for a while? As a matter of fact, clean up. I remember how clean you always were. And cook some damn food or something before I starve." He ended that statement with him getting up and throwing a broom at me.

"Don't worry. Start with the cleaning, and I will call for some groceries. I want lobster tails and shrimp with rice and corn for dinner. Oh, and bake me some shit, a cake or something. A nigga been waiting to have you back in my hold for so long, baby, you don't even know."

Not really knowing what to do at this point, I took the broom and made my way to the kitchen, praying some cleaning supplies existed in this place because I was not trying to piss Noah's bipolar ass off. Seeing some dish soap, Ajax, an old sponge, and half a bottle of bleach, I began soaking dishes and sweeping the floors. I knew he wouldn't let me leave, but I wasn't leaving without killing him for killing Kadia anyway. Once Phantom found him and figured out what happened to Kadia, he would kill him for me. *But what if he doesn't come or it's too late and I am dead?* I was only running away if I had to save the baby I was carrying. I would not allow another of my children to come to harm.

Thinking about Kadia being dead brought tears to my eyes, and I began to sob. I didn't even care that I was leaning up against a wall that was dirtier than the ground.

Pushing on, I began to clean again. *I have to still be strong.* Noah liked to play games, so maybe Kadia wasn't dead or even hurt. *Maybe Phantom saved her already, or maybe Phantom took her and is just playing a trick on me. So many maybes. I wish I called Lox before this. I trust him, and he would have helped. I was really behaving stupid, but if I get out of this, I will do better in the future.*

Hearing a loud knock at the door, I stopped in my tracks, hoping I would hear Kadia's voice or maybe Noah would leave and I could find something to kill him with later. There had to be a hammer or a knife somewhere in this raggedy-ass house. Seeing him snatch some bags from some chick, I could hear her whining to him.

"Noah, why can't I come in? I hope you are not cheating on me. I love you, and you are treating me so bad." Her fucking voice was giving me a headache, and I wished she would go on. *If she ain't talking about the whereabouts of my kid, then she got to go.*

"Look, babe, I know you miss me, and I miss you too. I'ma come check you tomorrow. You know I am spending time with my daughter right now. Remember you seen her the other day? I can't have you hanging with us because her mom is a bitch and won't let me see her anymore if I do. Just keep it tight for your man, and I'ma come bless you soon." With that said, Noah kissed the girl, snatched the grocery bags, and made his way to me.

"I didn't tell you stop cleaning. Here is the groceries. Get to cooking so I can have a full belly. I need all my energy when I tear that shit up tonight." When he turned his back to me, I wanted to throw one of the bags at his head.

Before long, I had cleaned all of downstairs and cooked the requested seafood dish and a red velvet cake for dessert. I learned to cook from my grandma when I was younger, and it was something I actually loved doing. Kadia and I would bake a ton of desserts for the holidays. She always loved helping me out in the kitchen. There were so many things I loved about my daughter. I mean, yes, she used to get on my nerves sometimes, what kid didn't? But she was my whole world. I couldn't imagine a day without her.

"What the fuck you in here thinking about? I hope you ain't put shit in the food. As a matter of fact, you 'bout to eat this shit too, so make a plate." He came in talking shit. *What the fuck he think I am in here thinking about? Our fucking daughter, the most important person in my life. What would any other mother be thinking about at a time like this?* I didn't poison his food because I knew he would be too smart for that and I would end up eating that shit first.

After we ate, I saw him grabbing at his crotch and looking my way. I had barely been here a day, and now I was going to be forced to have sex with his ass. I tried to blend in with the dusty couch, hoping he would call whoever he was talking to at the door earlier, but no such luck. He grabbed me by both arms, pinning me down and kissing all over me with his big lips. It felt like he was slobbering on me. How could I have ever thought that he was attractive? How did he even turn me on enough to get me pregnant?

Trying to fight him, I kicked him, but he turned, and my little knee hit his ribs instead. Irritated by me, he slammed my body down on the couch again, and my head snapped back. He used force to rip my clothes off, and then he forced his way in. I could feel my pussy bleeding, not because he was big but because he was rough. My nose was bleeding too from him slamming my head around. I began praying. *Lord, please, I am praying for my unborn child, not for myself. Please do not allow Noah to harm my unborn child.*

Eventually he stopped, but this continued over the next few days. He would have sex with me in the worst manner. He tied me up today and raped me in my ass. I shit and bled all over, and after he came all over my back, he told me to hurry and clean up.

As soon as he said that, there was knocking at the door. I wondered if a neighbor heard me screaming and called the police. Seeing him cautiously move to the door and peek out of the window, I heard him curse low. Standing me up and shoving me into the downstairs closet, he warned me, "Stay fucking quiet, or I will kill you the minute you speak." I could tell by the look on his face that he was serious, too.

Looking around the small closet, I saw an old pillow that looked yellowed with age and a rough brown blanket. It smelled like pee, and I wondered who Noah had locked up in here like an animal before me. Scooting back some so I could try to get comfortable and rest while I was away from him, I felt something metal. Holding it up into the light in the crack of the door, I gasped out loud. It was Kadia's Pandora bracelet from Phantom.

She never took it off. Even when she went to sleep, I would have to remove it from her wrist after she was out for the night. I still remembered the day Phantom gave it to her. It was after we came back from seeing Azia and his Aunt Sena. Kadia went to her first day of summer camp and came home with a certificate for being a good friend. The next day Phantom picked her up from camp in the Bentley which was, for some reason, Kadia's favorite car of his to ride in, and he had the bracelet and a bouquet of flowers waiting for her in the back seat. She was so happy she smiled like never before. She came home holding the bracelet in her hand, jumping around the room until Sahnai and I asked what she had.

She had said, "Mommy, it's the best gift ever. My very own big girl bracelet, and there is a princess crown on it and a teddy bear and a sparkly letter K. K is for Kadia. It has all of my favorite colors: blue, pink and purple." She put it on and that was it. No other bracelet was worn again or even talked about. I asked Phantom why he would get a 4-year-old such an expensive gift, and he said he wanted her to not have to look for a man to treat her good and give her stuff when she had her daddy to do it. That was how little girls got mixed up with the wrong kind of men.

Listening to Noah, I was shaken out of my memories when I recognized the other voice in the room with him. It was his mother, Mocha. She was something else, and I always thought she controlled him for the most part. If anything, he was scared of her even as a grown-ass man. After they argued about something I didn't hear all the way, the noises sounded like sex noises. I was confused. Did she come in with his so-called girlfriend from the other night?

"Noah, I seen you fucking her when I got here today, and I am pissed. This is why I wanted to get rid of Kadia, because I knew you were still lusting after her mother. I have been telling you this for years. I don't want to share you with anyone. Your full focus, time, love, and attention should always be on me and only me."

"Mom, seriously? You knew I wanted Inaya when you took Kadia out of here. What did you think I was going to do?"

"Your stupid-ass baby mother stole her, Noah. That is what I came over here to tell you before I lost my train of thought watching you and that slut having sex. Toya snuck her out after I let her and Lallani come for a visit. So since I cannot kill Kadia, Lallani will have to go and her simple mother too."

"Mom, why would you want to hurt Lallani? She is my oldest daughter, and I want you to leave her alone. I don't see her, so you should have no problem with her at all. I don't know why you keep pretending to be the loving grandmother to see her from time to time. Are you making sure we have no relationship? I fucking told you we don't. I mean it. Leave Lallani alone!"

"Aww, Noah, you want me to leave her alone like you wanted me to leave your little sister alone? Yeah, I made sure you left Tameka alone. I remember how you used to look at her, all the love you had in your eyes when you watched her. I made sure I took care of that little home wrecker. She thought she could win your love and you would love her more than me. When I shoved her down the basement stairs, she never knew what happened. She trusted me because I was her mother." Mocha finished with a crazy-ass laugh.

"You killed my sister? Because you thought she wanted to do what with me? She was five. You are sick. I hate you, and I want you to get the fuck away from me," Noah screamed. After that I heard the front door slam, and then it was quiet. I guessed Noah left after that whole embarrassing scene. *Wow. His mother has to be his lover or something. She is sick. She killed his baby sister because she was that jealous. Toya? Wait, the same Toya who is supposed to be pregnant by Phantom? This is too many coincidences, but my baby is alive. I can't believe it. I have to get out of here and get home to her.* I was going to rest, then figure out how to get out.

A few hours later, I felt cold air touch my skin, and I heard the door creak slowly open.

"Get up, little girl. It is time for you to get out of here and not come back."

Looking into the face of Miss Mocha, aka Noah's mom, I was scared that she was there and he was not, but she threw a clean white T-shirt at me and the bag of money I brought.

"Noah is not here. Hurry up and leave right now. A taxi is waiting for you at the corner, and when you make it home, take your little devil child and go far away. I don't want either of you around my son. If not, I will kill you both," she threatened as she ushered me to the front door.

Not waiting for her to change her mind, I grabbed the bag and threw the shirt on as I ran as fast as my bruised and battered body would let me to the corner. Seeing the taxi, I almost cried with relief.

"I need to go to Garden of Elmwood in Brighton. Do you have a phone I can borrow?" I asked the friendly looking taxi driver. He was an old man, maybe in his sixties, with all-white hair and a very concerned look on his face.

"Ma'am, would you like me to call the police or take you to a hospital?"

"Please, I just want to call my husband to see if our daughter is okay first, then yes, I do need to get to a hospital, I guess."

He reluctantly handed me his cell phone. I dialed Phantom and prayed he answered the unfamiliar number. It rang to voicemail, and I burst into tears. I tried the business line that he told me to call in an emergency, and he finally picked up.

"Yo, who the fuck is this playing on my phone?"

"Phantom, it's me, Inaya. Please tell me you have Kadia with you."

"Iny, where the fuck are you? Stay right there. I'ma come get you, ma. Is my fucking baby okay? I'ma kick your tiny ass when I see you for leaving and not telling me shit."

"Phantom, I am in a taxi near Clifford and Joseph. I am going to have him take me to the hospital over here. Please come meet me. I am in pain, and I am scared. I think the baby is okay, but I want to make sure. I am sorry. I was trying to save Kadia, and Noah tricked me." I began crying hysterically as the taxi started to drive me to Rochester General Hospital, and Phantom stayed on the phone trying to calm me down. As I pulled up and ended the call with him, he assured me he and Kadia were on the way.

I walked slowly to the emergency door, so happy to be free and to know that my daughter was safe but scared to know if my baby was okay. If something was wrong with the baby, it would have been all my fault.

Chapter 33

Noah

Sitting in my car, waiting for this nigga Cudjie in the Walmart parking lot, I replayed the videos of me having sex with Inaya. I could feel myself getting hard, and my man was making a tent in my gray sweatpants. Looking around and not seeing anyone parked next to me, I pressed play on the video of me busting Inaya's ass open, and at the same time I took my dick out and used my left hand to jack off. Yes, I could still remember how tight her ass was as I slid inside, and hearing her screams and her begging me to stop turned me on even more. It only took a few minutes before I was oozing cum all down my hand and boxers. Grabbing a rag from the passenger seat, I cleaned myself up and sanitized my hand after pulling my pants up.

Seeing Cudjie pull up in a red Nissan Altima, I hopped out to meet him halfway. "Hey, what's good?"

"Shit, I can't call it. You got the pretty bitch over there locked up and playing your sex slave, so you tell me."

"Man, my moms let the fucking kid get rescued by my other baby moms, so now my whole plan is fucked up. I hope Kadia doesn't end up with Phantom, because she is smart, and I cannot chance him finding me with Inaya. He will kill me. I can tell he loves her, and I know he is ruthless, so I am moving her tonight. I think I may head to Canada and chill out for a while, so I am going to need all that bread you owe me now."

"Did you send him the pictures and videos of Inaya?" Cudjie asked, not addressing my request for money owed.

Showing him my phone so he could see the sent message to Phantom, I confirmed I sent it to him. "See? He got all of them, and I even see the read receipt, so I know they were read."

"So he never responded at all?"

"Naw, he didn't say a word. Maybe he is no longer interested in her now that I violated her the way I did. I know I wouldn't want any female for a wife after the stuff I did," I said, laughing.

"A'ight, cool, well, a deal is a deal, so here is your money, and have a safe trip to Canada," he said, handing me a duffel bag with money in it. Before I could take it out and count it, he was already peeling out of the store parking lot. After counting the money two times and seeing that it was getting late, I came to the final conclusion that Cudjie's snake ass shorted me five grand. Honestly, I was not surprised. That was what I got for dealing with a shady-ass nigga like him. I mean, he was getting off on hurting his brother and paying for it. If I had a brother, I wouldn't be doing that shit. I have to let it go, because as much as I be slapping these bitches around, I tried not to fight these dudes. My smile was too perfect to be injured in a fight.

Turning the key in the car, I decided it was time to go home and check on my little prize. Maybe today I would make her swallow my cum. I had been saving that as a kind of celebration, so since I got paid, it was the perfect timing. Pulling up to the house, I noticed my mom's little green smart car parked in the driveway. "Fuck," I said to myself, wondering what she wanted now. Walking to the door, I noticed it was already unlocked. *How did she get in when she doesn't have a key?* She was so sneaky and had been my whole life.

As soon as I walked in the living room and saw her sitting there with that fucked-up lipstick and a smirk on her face, I knew there was about to be some shit. "Well, hello to you too, son. How nice of you to greet your mother with kind words and a kiss," she sarcastically said.

Walking by her and toward the closet as fast as I could, I stopped, noticing the door was opened slightly. Pushing it all the way open and looking inside, I could see that Inaya was gone.

Running back to the living room, I couldn't help but to grab my mom by her collar. "Where is Inaya? Where is she?" I yelled in her face.

Not even flinching, she responded in her annoyingly calm voice. "I didn't kill her, so let go of me now. I let her go, but if I catch her or that little brat of yours around again, I will kill them. I told you I will not share you with anyone, and I meant it. Now I am going to go cook you a nice meal, and then we can cuddle."

As she pushed me to the side and walked toward the kitchen, I sank to my knees and put my head in my hand. *What is wrong with me? I am a monster, but it is not my fault.* She made me this way. She made me hate women. I was still trying to come to terms with the information she gave me yesterday about her killing the one girl I loved unconditionally: my little sister.

I wished someone had saved me and Tameka when we were small, because we truly needed saving. My mother thought I was her boyfriend. She cuddled with me. Kissed me on my mouth and even had sex with me sometimes. The bad part was that I liked having sex with her. She was my first and knew exactly what I liked. Being around her made me feel disgusting. I knew what she had been doing to me all these years was wrong.

Growing up, I didn't have a normal childhood that I could remember. I always slept in my mother's bed. Even when she had a boyfriend, she wouldn't let him sleep over because that was our special time. She would snuggle up to me all night, kissing my neck and stroking my hair. I would go to school, but I was not allowed to go to friends' houses or have them over, so by the time I turned 12, I stopped talking to other kids because it was a waste of time. When I turned 15, my mother bought me an eight ball of cocaine and taught me how to bag it up and told me I was now the man of the house, so I should be taking care of her. She sent me outside and told me not to come back until I sold everything. I then became a drug dealer, but not by choice. I wanted to be an astronaut. When my dream died was when I began to hate my mother.

In high school, I met a few girls and would try to date them, but my mom always ran them away, saying I couldn't speak to them because they were not good enough for me. But then I met Toya. She didn't let my mother scare her away at all. My mom went so far as to fight Toya when she caught us fucking in my room after school one day. She beat her like she was another grown woman, but the next morning Toya was at my locker waiting for me with a hug and a smile. By the time we found out Toya was pregnant with Lallani, my mother had stopped by the school to drop off my physical forms, and while she was there, she broke into Toya's locker, planting drugs. After a quick call to the police and the principal with an anonymous tip, my mother finally got her way. Toya had our daughter in jail, and when she came home, she wanted nothing else to do with me or my crazy-ass family. I was the reason Toya's life as an adult got off to such a fucked-up start. She was the reason Inaya's was fucked up too. She made me treat the women

I loved with cruelty because that was what she taught me. She made me hate my own children.

Hearing my mother hum her favorite song, the one about the blue bird, made the anger inside of me boil. My mother would never let me go. *Look at how she allowed Inaya to leave me. She will always be here to ruin my life if I don't do something right now.* Grabbing the gun, I made my way to the kitchen to do what I should have done a long time ago. I was going to kill my mother.

Chapter 34

Sahnai

Being home from the hospital really made me appreciate my bed and real food so much more than I used to. Not only was the place cold, the bed lumpy, and the staff rude, but after Lox walked out on me, he brought his mom up to bring li'l Q in to see me once, and I had not seen or heard from him since. I cried the last four days I was there because I wanted my son, but I knew in my heart I could not manage him by myself right now. At least now if I had to cry, I could do that shit in the privacy of my home. Feeling my side hurt like crazy when I walked and knowing I was still filled with stitches and bandages, I had trouble breathing when I moved around. It just made me angry at the situation all over again. I wished I could have seen the person who did this to me. I was too busy picking up the pieces of my broken heart to notice what was going on around me. The blade struck right below my ribs, and that was the wound that hurt the most. Thank God the kids were not hurt in the attack and Lox was there to call for help, or I may not even be here right now.

I didn't know how I was going to take care of myself like this. I pissed off Lox, and I thought my cousin was still missing somewhere. I tried to call Dana when I heard she was in town to see if she wanted to come stay with me and help out, but she kept sending me to voice-mail. I guessed she was mad on behalf of her brother or some dumb shit. I called Azia, but she was in the hospital with Kadia still so my grandma could go home. I guessed when I needed someone, they all said fuck me. I bet stupid fucking Inaya was not even missing. All this talk about Noah abusing her and Kadia must have been a bag of lies, because I never heard that before, and she used to tell me everything. She probably left Canada and Noah because he told her to go. I was sure he found someone else, a girl who was not so whiny and needy.

Drying off with my beach-size blue Victoria's Secret towel, I began to apply lotion to my skin: Cherry Blossom from Bath & Body Works. *Yeah, that has to be it. Inaya ran off with Noah because she begged him to come and be with her. Maybe he felt sorry for her. I mean, she is cute, but not beautiful like me. Well, like I was until my body became all scarred and shit.* Pulling out an orange and green American Eagle tee and some gray tights, I put them on with some tall colored socks to match. Grabbing my brown fur throw blanket, I made my way downstairs.

Making myself some shrimp and rice, I sat down on my red leather couch to eat. Turning on the sixty-inch TV in the living room, I began peeling my orange and flipped through the channels. I thought it was a mistake coming back here since it resulted in me almost losing my life and me basically losing my son. *As soon as I get better, I am going to find a way to fuck up Lox for keeping my son away from me, and I am going to take my son away, and he will not be seeing him again.* We were doing all right until Lox came in the picture, and his little ratchet baby mama could know she would be getting it, too.

I must have fallen asleep because I woke up to my phone ringing off the hook and about twenty missed calls and even more unread texts. A lot of them were from a number I didn't know. Opening a message, I saw it was Honest.

202-521-4456 3:45 p.m.: Sahnai, I came up here to get you. I can see you not ready to come home right away, but you need to let me know where you at so I can come and be there, because this hotel life ain't shit. Plus, I am your nigga, so I need to be where you at. I don't trust that light-skin-ass nigga you say is your baby daddy. Don't think I am forgetting that shit about you fucking him either. I'ma punish your little ass for that when you feel better.

202-521-4456 5:30 p.m.: Yo, I know you see me calling you and messaging you. What the fuck? Don't make me do no stalker shit and track your fucking phone. Hit me back wit' the address, and let me come take care of you, bae. I love you and miss you, so hit me back.

I also had messages from Lox, Dana, Azia, and Phantom. Deciding to at least call Phantom's crazy ass back before he drove over here, I dialed him first.

"Yo, Sahnai, why the fuck you not answering your phone and shit? What if something was wrong wit' li'l Q or Inaya? Anyway, I don't have time to lecture you on how to be decent or a good mom or person. I need a favor. Actually this shit is not for me. It's for Kadia. So while you over there mad at the fucking world, I know you got love for her. Inaya is still missing, and you are listed as Kadia's emergency contact for everything. I need to get her checked out of here, so you have to come check her out. Can you at least do that?"

Not even hesitating, I knew I was agreeing. I loved Kadia. I didn't know why I was even mad at Inaya. I just was, but that shit had nothing to do with Kadia.

"Of course I will sign her out, and she can come stay with me, too, until her mom comes back. I am her god-mother and cousin, so I will always be here for her. And, Phantom, like always, you being an asshole. I didn't get my missed calls because I was asleep. I am on pain meds because your and Lox's bitch stabbed me up. I would always answer when it comes to my kid and my family. Is she still at Strong? I can drive up there since I am at home."

"You know what, ma? You right. I know you was stabbed up by some unknown person, since you said you didn't see a face. I'ma send Azia to come and grab you so you don't have to drive." With that shit being said, he hung right up.

Calling Lox back next, I got no answer, so I figured Q was good, or Phantom would have said something. Texting Honest back, I sent him my address and let him know I was going to take care of some family shit, but he should check me later.

I went and brushed my teeth and washed my face. Not bothering to change, I threw a hoodie on and some Jordan slides. Before I could even make it back downstairs, I heard a car horn blowing. Fuck, Azia couldn't even bring her ass to the door to see if I needed help. Stepping out of the house and walking to the silver Benz truck she was driving, I was feeling the pain but not wanting to look like a punk. I stood straight and climbed in without even making a face.

"Hey, Azia girl, you look stressed. Kadia is home now, so at least that is something to look happy about. Or is your crazy-ass brother stressing you out?"

"Naw. I am worried about Inaya. I am surprised you are not," she replied with a rude-ass attitude. Deciding not to argue with her since I was in no position to defend myself, I just shrugged my shoulders and looked out the window at the trees and houses and shit. *She is probably just miserable because she ain't got no man, and I know how I get when I am not being fucked right.*

Pulling up in the hospital parking garage, we parked and went to the pediatrics floor. It took a little longer than I thought to sign Kadia out. A social worker wanted to speak to me and get details on all the bruises and cuts that happened. I felt scared for Inaya for the first time as I heard the list of shit Noah had damaged on my little cousin. She even had bruised ribs, which she assured me would heal in about two weeks. Kadia was happy to see me. I had to tell her to be careful when hugging me, but this was the best part of my day. Lox even brought Q up to the hospital to see me for a little while.

While we all got ready to walk out, I wondered who was taking me home.

"Sahnai, me and Q will take you home, ma. Come on, let me hold your arm. You look like you in pain and shit." I appreciated Lox's help. I was in pain now since the kids wanted to hug me and jump on me.

As soon as we got to the car, he even opened the door for me and helped me in.

"Look, Sahnai, when we get to the house, let's talk. I am sorry about what you thought you saw with Toya. If you let me explain how she saved Kadia and I was just giving her money to get away from Noah, you would understand. He is her daughter's father, and his mother and him are into some weird shit. Basically, she thinks they are coming for her kid next. I couldn't let that shit happen to another little girl, ma. You understand. I don't want that bitch though. I only love you."

I didn't respond, but I slid my hand into his and laid my head on his shoulder while he drove us home. As soon as we pulled up, I was confused by the green Ford Explorer parked in my driveway. The windows were tinted, so I couldn't see who was inside. Stepping out slowly with Lox next to me, I noticed he had his gun pulled and by his side.

"Yo, what the fuck you get out for?" he whispered harshly. Before I could defend my actions, I saw Honest jump out of the truck and walk toward me.

"Yeah, I came just in time. Baby daddy my ass, Sahnai. I just told your ass today stop fucking playing wit' me. Now get your ass in the house so I can make you feel better," he said while grabbing my arm and smirking at Lox. I could tell he was waiting for me to fix this situation, but I didn't know how.

"Lox, thanks for the ride. Call me later, and we can talk about when Q can come home." He turned at the last word I spoke and jumped in his car before he sped down the road like a madman. "Damn."

Chapter 35

Inaya

Looking around my house with Kadia in my arms, I started crying again. This baby was making me an emotional mess. I was also crying because Phantom had done so much to make sure the house was clean and that I would be comfortable when I got home. I knew they wanted me to stay in the hospital, but I needed to be near my daughter and Azia. The nightmares were terrible, and I needed to know that Kadia was safe. Plus, I wanted to check on Sahnai and make sure she was okay and tell her I was sorry I wasn't there when she woke up. Azia told me about her and Lox beefing, and I didn't really know what to say. She was always doing some bullshit, especially where Lox was concerned. She was taking this shit too far, especially with this Honest nigga, but she was my cousin, so I was going to support her no matter what, right or wrong. I was surprised she didn't come see me in the hospital, but maybe she was not able. I really didn't know how she was doing physically.

Not wanting to stay here, I left Kadia with Azia and the boys downstairs and went to take a shower so I could pack my bags and go next door with her. Feeling the hot water beat down on me, I began to sing a love song I made up. I liked writing music and singing it especially. It soothed me and made me feel calm. Ending the song with the line, "Because I love you," I pulled back the shower curtain to reach for my white thick towel and almost had a heart attack when I noticed Phantom sitting on the toilet seat watching me.

"Ahh," I screamed, startled, and I began to trip over the side of the tub. Feeling his arms around me, catching me so I didn't fall, left me not knowing how to feel.

I missed this touch, but I didn't know if I could trust him after all that had happened and all the stories Noah and Cudjie told me. Even if none of what they said was true, which I kind of figured out on my own, I had to remember that Phantom ended our friendship/fuckship, whatever it was that we had before all of this. I didn't want to get close to him and get hurt again, and I sure as hell didn't want him to be with me now because of pity. While I was in the hospital, he didn't leave my side unless he was taking Kadia, Azia, and the boys back and forth from hospital to home. He slept in the chair next to my bed every night and watched bullshit on TV with me when I couldn't sleep. He even climbed in bed a few times to hold me when I woke up from having nightmares. I thought he only did all of that because the baby I was carrying was his.

Now that everyone knew I was pregnant, they all treated me like glass. It was annoying but true. With all the shit that had happened lately, I guessed I couldn't blame them.

"Babe, you okay?" Phantom asked me while carrying me to the bedroom and getting my lotion off the dresser. I felt so much better after a real shower with a lot of hot water. I took the Marc Jacobs lotion and mixed it with the liquid baby oil, then rubbed my body down. I was surprised that Phantom wasn't trying to get some or at least cop a feel. Maybe he heard me and the doctor when he talked about how I was raped and how I had some minor damage to my kitty cat.

Sliding my white and pink lace bra on with a matching thong, I caught Phantom staring at me, except the look on his face wasn't one of lust. It was an intense look I could not place, but I was sure he was disgusted with me now. He would never want these damaged goods again, and I could understand that. Sadly, I hurried and put on a lime green sweat suit from Pink with gold writing. I threw my feet into a pair of pink house slippers and got ready to go stay next door.

"Phantom, can you help me with my bags so I can go next door and lie down? This baby is sucking the energy out of me, and I have to try to get some rest. I want to stay with Azia if you don't mind. I miss her, and no telling when she will be going back home."

He grabbed my stuff and responded, "Ma, my crib is your crib, so you and Kades stay as long as you want."

Once I made my way next door after locking up my place, I stepped in the door to a lot of little hugs. All of Azia's boys, li'l Q, and Kadia ran to me, calling my name all at the same time. "Yo, none of y'all better not be squishing my baby. Back up," Phantom yelled, moving kids off of me. It made me laugh to see how serious he was being over this. Leaning down and kissing everyone, I went to sit with Azia at the kitchen breakfast bar. I could hear my stomach making noise, but I did not see any food being cooked.

"So, umm, sis, you not 'bout to cook for me or nothing? I mean, I am carrying your little greedy-ass niece or nephew."

"Sis, what you want? We will make Phantom and Lox go get it because I ain't cooking shit today."

After we sent the guys and kids out to go pick up some Chipotle—I was craving a steak bowl with extra sour cream—Azia and I moved to the couch and turned on the latest episode of *Catfish*. Laughing and making plans for tomorrow to go to the movies with the kids, I started feeling sad.

"Azia, I am going to miss you when you go back to Connecticut. I wish I had the money to move up there so we could hang out more," I pouted.

"Aww, sis, I am actually gonna move down here. My aunt is gonna be here until God knows when since Lox got two kids and no help, and I miss my brother. Plus, I want to be here with you and Kadia and the new baby. Inaya, you are like the sister I always wanted. Growing up with Lox and Phantom was a challenge being the only girl. Me and you are like best friends. As soon as you learn to spend up all of Phantom's money in the mall like me, we will be like twins."

"Azia, I feel the same way. I remember being so nervous to meet you, and once I did, we just clicked. I used to be so close to my cousin growing up, but she always had a lot of times she just pushed me away or got angry with me for reasons I couldn't figure out. I have never had a person who always had my back the way you have, and I really appreciate you. Plus, I admire you. You're a great mom, and you're so strong and smart. I don't know what I would do with three boys. Wait, do twins run in your side or in your baby father's side? Because this better only be one damn baby," I asked, making an ugly fake-cry face.

"Girl, nope. In my baby father's side of the family, so you safe. And stop with all the appreciation. You gonna make me cry. I think we are too close. Your hormones are rubbing off on me."

"Girl, no tears. Let's talk about where you want a house and what kind. I hope you get a pool. We love to swim and there is no pool here. Oooh, and you should get a Jacuzzi in the backyard and maybe some fruit trees. I love oranges. Maybe we can import an orange tree."

"Girl, your pregnant ass just thinking about nothing but food. I am surprised you didn't have an opinion on the kitchen and what food to buy. Anyway, I am thinking about moving into the Reserve where Lox just moved. They have brand new houses being built in there, and it's on a cul-de-sac. I went there the first time and fell in love with the place. It has high ceilings and marble everything, and there are even fireplaces. Oh, yeah, and yes, a pool and a Jacuzzi. If worse comes to worst, we going to stay in Lox's house. Once I sell the house in Jersey, I will have enough to buy three of those houses up here. Cost of living is so low compared to where I am at."

We talked for a while longer about her buying all new furniture and how much fun we were going to have decorating the house and the yard.

"Azia, what about Lox's sister? Are you two close?" I asked with a little feeling of jealousy.

"No, we are not close really, even though we grew up in the same house for about twelve years. I don't know why. I guess partly because I have a whole family and she is still a teenager. She is only seventeen. Another reason is she has always been kind of strange. It seems like she is not close to anyone in the family, and she has no respect for Aunt Sena."

"Wow, that's fucked up. I hope she outgrows that and learns to respect her mother."

The guys walked in with our Chipotle, and I almost snatched the whole bag out of Phantom's hand.

"What took so long? I am about to starve to death. I almost started to eat the arm of the sofa," I joked.

"Kadia wanted Popeye's, so we made another stop." Rolling my eyes at both Lox and Phantom, who looked like they were both guilty as hell, I sat down to tear my steak bowl up. "Damn, shawty, slow down. You gonna choke or some shit. You want me to grab you a bib?"

Giving Phantom the bird, I didn't stop or even look up. *See, when he is being nice, he and I just flow. But before long he will be treating me like a fucking dummy again, making choices that will hurt me in the long run. It's best if I just continue to stay away from him.*

Watching him play with the kids and talk shit to Azia, all I could do was smile. When I was locked up in the closet of Noah's little hideaway in the hood, all I could think about were Kadia and Phantom. I missed them so much.

Once the kids all fell asleep, he and Lox came downstairs in all black. I knew they were going to kill Noah. He talked to me about it earlier today. He had him in some secure location with some people torturing him since the day I was let go. I was really surprised he had not made it over there yet to finish him off, but Lox told me Phantom didn't want to leave my side.

Phantom told me when they came to grab Noah's bitch ass, he was holding his mother, who was bleeding everywhere, in his arms saying he was sorry. I guessed he couldn't take the sick obsession she had for him, and in some sick way, maybe he was trying to save his daughter from the same fate as his sister, so he killed her.

Waiting for Phantom to lean down and kiss my cheek before he walked out the door, I made up my mind again. *I got to stay away from this man.*

Chapter 36

Lox

Pulling up to Walmart, I wished I had taken my mom's offer to watch the kids, but I had to learn how to function with my two boys by myself. She wouldn't always be here, and I didn't trust any strangers. Struggling to set the baby seat in the back of the cart and li'l Q in the seat part, I was already tired and frustrated, and we hadn't even bought shit yet. *Yo, I don't know how moms do this shit on their own for real, but they get my respect a hundred. Not sure what the fuck I should be getting for these kids and me.* I decided to start with diapers.

Grabbing some size-three diapers—my mom made sure to write that shit down for Aiden—I then went and got baby wipes, some Gerber juices, and baby food. Going to the snack aisle, I decided to get some chips and shit for Q. Just a few things, but this nigga was grabbing everything and throwing it in the cart. Shit was hitting his brother's seat and overflowing onto the floor.

"Yo, Qualyl, Daddy said a few things. Stop touching stuff, my man." He decided Daddy was a joke when he snatched a huge bag of popcorn from a nearby shelf. Snatching it back, I put it on the shelf, and he started screaming.

"I want it!"

Shit, he's big. He can have that tantrum if he wants to. Then Aiden started crying. *What the fuck. They can't wait until I am home to start all that crying and shit?* Pulling out my phone, I thought about calling my mom to ask what to do, because Aiden was turning red and people were staring at me.

"Bad daddy. Daddy, you're mean. I want the popcorn," Q yelled in his little voice, which seemed very loud in this store filled with people.

"Hey, Lox, you need some help?" I heard a voice filled with laughter ask me. Turning around, I saw Alani. She was a cool-ass chick Phantom and I knew because we used to do business with her baby father from time to time. Actually, he was our gun supplier. Unfortunately, he got caught fucking someone else's woman in their house and lost his life. The couple of years we hadn't seen Alani had been good to her. She was looking like a fucking angel. Her natural curly hair was pulled back in a head band, and her mocha-colored skin was shining like she was out for a run or something. She smelled like peaches. I swore that shit was my favorite fruit. I just wanted a damn taste.

"Oww. Yo, Q, chill for real, dude," I spoke up after he threw a can of peas at me, hitting me in the foot. "Alani, you just came into my life like an angel come to save me from these crazy kids. Please help. I will pay you, hug you, whatever you need," I joked but was half serious.

Picking up Aiden first, she bounced him a few seconds before he snuggled down into her shoulder, smiling at me with his hand in his mouth and drool flying everywhere. Then she handed Q a small bag of chips I already had in the cart, opened them, and wiped his tears. Just like that it was over, and I could head to the checkout.

"So, Alani, what's been up? Shit, I haven't seen you in forever, ma. How is princess Vivian? She still a diva?"

"Shit, Lox, she is still a diva for real. She will be six this year and be walking around the house in my fur coat and high heels, singing them damn songs to the movie *Frozen* into a toy microphone. Some day she is gonna be famous, but for now I guess I am her audience," she replied with a smile on her face.

"That's cool, ma. What about you? How you been? I came looking for you to check on you a few times, but you had moved out of the spot in Chili."

"Yeah, after all that shit wit' Travis, I had to get my head right. The girl he was cheating with ended up being pregnant and was coming by my shit harassing me. I didn't want Vivy to have to see or hear that, so I moved to stay wit' my mom in Miami for a year so I could finish school. Now that I've graduated, I was offered a job here, so I moved back. We live in this area now near Lehigh Station Road."

Collecting my change from the cashier who kept trying to flirt with me, I was kind of annoyed. *Some women have no class. She doesn't know if Alani and I are together, but she still brushing her hand up against mine, smiling all in my face.* Hell, her brave ass even asked me my name and wrote her number on my receipt. I started to let it go and just throw away her number, but seeing how pretty Alani was holding Aiden in her arms made me want to stick up for her.

"Yo, Shante, is it?" I asked the cashier with the purple box braids and low-cut white tee that she had the nerve to be cashiering in. Shit, I could see her whole bra through the tee. *Don't they have any fucking rules in this bitch?*

"Yes, babe?"

"First of all, I ain't your babe. Second, you really just did all of that, and I am standing here in line with a woman and two kids? You thought what, I was gonna disrespect my woman in front of her and our kids and give you some play? Shit, I wanna make it clear, I ain't calling you, and I don't allow bitches to disrespect my woman, so why don't you worry about the prices of the shit people are buying instead of being a fucking home wrecker?" I grabbed the cart and ushered Alani and the kids out the door.

Once we made it to the parking lot, she followed me to my white Audi. It seemed like I drove this the most because it was easier to put the kids in than the truck. Once they were in and quiet—I didn't know how she kept doing that—she turned to me.

"Well, damn, Lox, we not together. You could have hollered at the girl in there. You probably hurt her feelings or some shit." She was trying to keep a straight face, but I could see a smile hiding behind her tucked-in lips.

"Ma, fuck her on the real. I am trying to see what's up wit' you."

"Lox, you out here wit' two babies. I am sure there is a baby mama somewhere on the scene, and as you know, I already been through it before, and I am not with it again. I am good by myself. Now, Vivy is at my sister's house, so I have to grab her before it gets too late. It was nice to catch up wit' you. You looking good as always." When she said that and turned to walk away, I could see the lust-filled look she was giving me.

"Damn, Alani. No hug or nothing? No number so we can hang out? Maybe I want to check on Vivy and make sure she good. Look, I know my situation looks fucked up, but I am single wit' two kids. My moms is up here from the city helping me and shit, so her and my sister is the only females in the house. I want to see you again, so just give me your number. As a matter of fact, lemme see your phone." Snatching the phone from her hand, I called my phone so I could lock in her number and save my number in her phone. "Call me so I know you made it home safe, and bring Vivy over tomorrow. She can swim wit' the other kids. Phantom has a daughter almost her age, and his sister's kids are in town, too."

"Wait, a girl have a kid wit' evil-ass Phantom? I'ma come just to meet this female, because I know you lying. I still remember how he used to embarrass any girl he would fuck. If she tried to call out to him, he would tell all kinds of personal shit until she looked the other way."

"I know this shit is crazy, but Iny loves his mean ass, and they got a baby on the way. Call me when you get home, and don't play and make me come find you and shit," I warned, hugging her before I watched her walk to her whip. Smelling her peaches scent on me as I jumped in the car, I had to smile to myself. Something about Alani just touched my soul.

As soon as I made it to the crib, I saw a tearful message from Sahnai saying she missed the boys and she couldn't sleep and wanted to die if she couldn't be with her son. She ended the message by saying she never told that bitch-ass nigga to come to her house, and it wasn't what it looked like. Thinking about how much Q asked for his mom this week, I decided to try to give this shit one more go. Even though I had Alani on my mind, I told Sahnai to come through.

"Hey, Lox, thanks for letting me come spend time wit' you guys," Sahnai said as she stepped through the door, brushing by me and hugging Q like she wasn't gone a day. She had on a long maxi dress with green and white stripes and some silver Coach sandals. Her ass was looking right in that dress, but her attitude was already annoying me. She came in here like she was the queen of England or some shit. *She needs to learn to humble herself because this is not a good look.* Watching her play with the boys and watch cartoons with them until they fell asleep, I realized how late it was, and Alani had not even hit me to tell me she was good.

"Yo, I'ma take them up to put them to bed," I explained, grabbing Aiden first. After settling him in his crib, I texted Alani and waited a few minutes to see if she would respond, but after a couple of minutes I didn't get a thing. Calling her a few times after I stuck Q in his bed, I figured she may be sleeping or still at her sister's house, but just in case, I sent my homeboy Clay a link to run her number and get me an address. He was a computer nerd and worked in IT for some Fortune 500 company. *This nigga is always able to get me info just from a number. It's like magic.* He would have found Sahnai's ass when she left too, but she left her phone behind. I guessed she knew what was up, but Alani's little pretty ass thought I was playing. *I hope she don't think I give a fuck about her man being someone I used to know. I mean, he isn't coming back, and we did business together. We were not friends.* I wanted her back then, but I wasn't a disrespectful-ass nigga. I knew shit even she didn't know, and that dude was treating her worse than she could have imagined. As a matter of fact, I heard a rumor he had a kid with Toya's ho ass, too.

Coming out of Q's room, I could see a light on in mine. Walking in, I see Sahnai's ass lying on my bed playing with her pussy. *This bitch ain't shit. Like she doesn't know my mom and sister are here, and she just being fucking nasty and shit.* Even though I was kind of pissed, it'd been a minute since I had some pussy with all this craziness going on. Taking my dick out, I walked next to the bed and grabbed her head, leading her mouth to my man. Feeling her trying to pull back, I tightened my grip.

"You want this shit, right? Stop playing and suck your shit then," I instructed after she nodded her head yeah. *I'm no rapist or nothing, shit.*

Just when I was getting into it good, Sahnai's phone kept going off back to back. Ignoring it and making sure I busted down her throat, I pulled out and pulled my pants right back up, waiting to see what she was going to say or do. She never even looked my way as she ran to her purse and got the phone out of the bag.

"Hello, babes. I am sorry. Inaya needed me, and I ended up falling asleep. I will be there in the morning. I love you too, babe," she cooed into the phone before clicking off.

"Yo, Sahnai, you sneaky as fuck. You better call your nigga Honest back and tell him you on your way now. I'ma run to the bathroom, and when I get back, you better be out my fucking crib. Ya see me?" I turned to walk into the master bathroom, slamming the door in her face.

Chapter 37

Alani

Making my way to my car, I clicked the alarm and slid in my blue 2015 Chevy Cruz. Yep, no foreign cars for me, even though my baby's father used to be the man and left me and our daughter with some money. That was what people didn't understand. It was some money, not enough to last a lifetime. I had to worry about doctors' bills, school fees, savings, and someday her college and wedding. I decided to not be like a lot of the females around me and live a little more on the modest side. Yeah, I still carried a Louie bag, but I owned two, not twenty. I got my hair and nails done, but I still had money left from what her father left us, and it had been two years.

After Travis was murdered, I moved to Miami with my mom and didn't buy a car or nothing. I spent a chunk of my money to go to school for interior design, and after I graduated, I was hired by a company in Rochester that works with the local real estate companies. I basically set up houses with the real estate company's budget to make them look good for showings. It was fun with flexible hours, and the money was not bad. I was able to get a townhouse in a nice little community when I moved back, and Vivian and I were cool. I guessed you could say I was happy with my life right now. Well, I was until I saw Lox.

Seeing Lox brought back a lot of memories. He was always the man to me. He was sexy as fuck, tall, and cut in all the right places, and he had those dreamy eyes. I used to pray Travis would not catch me looking his way, because anyone could see I had a thing for him. When he would talk to me, I would blush and laugh like a little girl. The thing I really liked about him was how he had a kind heart. He would always come hang at the park with the guys and play soccer with all the little boys or shoot hoops with them. He even bought me a baby shower gift when I had Vivy. She still had it actually. It was a baby bangle with diamonds and the word "princess" engraved on it. I kept it in her jewelry box as a keepsake. He was just different. He wasn't rude like most of the niggas Travis hung around, and he wasn't crazy and evil like his cousin Phantom. Look at how he remembered my daughter's name after all this time. I dated a nigga in Miami who went to college with me, and after six months he kept calling my daughter Vantasia. I had to just let him go. He wasn't paying attention to anything that was important in my life.

Sigh. I guessed he was feeling me now, but after all the drama I went through with his cheating-ass friend before he died, I was all set. *I'ma find me a nice nine-to-five nigga and call it a day. I am not even going to call this nigga to let him know I made it in. I'ma just pretend his number got erased out of my phone. I know trouble when I see it, and Lennox is trouble.*

As soon as I got to my sister's house, she told me Vivy fell asleep, so I had to carry her heavy behind to the car. Pulling up to my house, I realized I was lonely. Seeing Lox reminded me of how much I missed having a man around to make me laugh or give me hugs, shit, to give me some good dick.

"Vivy, we are home. Wake up." I helped my baby in the house and put away the little bit of stuff I picked up from the store that Lox insisted on paying for. I looked at my phone one more time. *Should I just send him a text saying I am okay? You know what, no. I am going to avoid temptation.* Getting baby girl and myself ready for bed, I put the phone on the charger and cuddled up next to Vivy in my bed. I was startled out of my sleep by my phone going off several times. Picking up my iPhone 6, I saw five missed calls and a few text messages. The number was saved under the name My Nigga.

1:25 a.m. My Nigga: Yo, shawty, why you fucking playing and shit? You didn't even let me know if you made it home safe or what. Remember what I said. Don't make me come find you.

3:15 a.m. My Nigga: A'ight, Alani, now I am getting worried. I know you know I got connects and will show up at your doorstep if I don't get a response soon. Hit me back ASAP.

Wow, I can see the devil is testing me. Turning my phone off, I rolled over and tried to go back to sleep. Giving up on sleep, I decided to start my day. Keeping my phone off, I brushed my teeth and washed my face. Putting on my yoga clothes, I grabbed my mat and went to the living room to get in some relaxation/exercise and try to get my mind off of calling Lox and inviting him over for some sex. I mean, shit. Yep, I meant for some sex. As the sun began creeping through the window, I was startled by a pounding on my door. *What the fuck?* Only my mama and my sister knew where I lived. I'd only been back for three weeks.

Walking to the door and grabbing my steel baseball bat on the way, I looked out the curtain in the front to see a tall nigga with his head down and a red hoodie on. *What the fuck is some random-ass nigga doing pounding on my door at five in the morning?* Wondering if I should be mad or concerned, I yanked the door open, ready to cuss the person out on the other side. "Who the fuck—"

"See, Alani? You being fucking hardheaded. I told you let me know you home safe or I am coming to find you. You playing games, ma."

Looking into angry green eyes as soon as he lifted his head for me to see who it was, I almost peed myself. Standing in front of me was the object of all my dreams for many years in the past and all of last night. *Fuck.* I didn't even know what to say. I should have just texted his ass and then blocked him. Now I was dealing with the man in the flesh, and my flesh was silently screaming, *touch me.* I could picture his long fingers caressing my breasts and slapping my ass as he took it from behind. Looking to see if I could tell what he was working with through the basketball shorts he had on, I lost track of the fact I was standing at my front door in a sports bra and some yoga pants.

"You done raping me at the front door, ma? Shit, if you want to see it just ask." He laughed and moved closer to me. I could smell his Gucci cologne, and that was when I felt it. Damn, his dick felt like a small arm was in his pants. I was no longer intrigued. I was scared. Backing away a little, I began to stutter.

"Well, you seen me. I am good. Thanks for checking on me."

"Damn, ma, it's like that? I stay up all night worrying about you, drive over here to make sure you good, and you don't even let a nigga in. I mean, can I get breakfast or have you for breakfast, something?"

Not wanting to be rude and not really being able to ignore the sad puppy dog face he was giving me, I opened the door for him. "Sorry, come in. Let me make some breakfast before Vivy wakes up. You eat pork, right?" I hoped so because that was a deal breaker. I couldn't stand being with a fussy-ass nigga who didn't eat beef, pork, this food, and that food. It was a headache.

"That's cool. I love to eat, and pork is food too. I don't discriminate," he said as he took off his Nike slides at the door and threw himself on my all-white leather sofa.

"Well, make yourself at home. Oh, wait, you already did."

"Just hurry up and cook, and then go get you and Vivy dressed. You're coming wit' me today. Bring your bathing suits, too," he threw at me as I walked to the kitchen trying to hide the smile on my face.

Chapter 38

Sahnai

Calling Inaya, I hoped she answered me. I really needed someone to talk to. Ever since that night I fucked up with Lox when Honest wouldn't stop blowing me up, he only let me see Q at my grandmother's house with her home for an hour here and there. When he first started this shit, I thought it was a joke, and I also felt like I had the upper hand because I was his mother so he couldn't just take him. I went to enforce my rights last Monday and was told since no one had had custody since he was born, and Lennox's name was on the birth certificate, whoever's care he was in was the primary guardian. If I didn't want him with his father, I had to take him to court.

Hearing Inaya's line ringing, I crossed my fingers that she would answer when she saw me calling.

"Hello."

"Hey, Inaya. Girl, I have been so tired from these pain meds I have not even been to check on you or call to check on you. I am so sorry. I just wanted to call and see if you are okay and see if Kadia is doing better."

"Yeah, I am good, and so is my baby and Kadia. Thanks for your concern." I couldn't tell if she was being sarcastic or serious when she thanked me.

"Baby? Girl, you're pregnant? Wow. By who? Is it Noah's?"

"Hell no, it is not Noah's baby. It is Phantom's baby, and yes, I am pregnant. I found out the day you were stabbed. Anyway, what have you really been up to?"

"On the real, cuz, my ex from DC is in town and won't leave me alone. I only gave him a chance because Lox was making out with Toya right outside my hospital room door, and I got mad because the nigga broke my heart. Now he is on all kinds of bullshit and won't let me have my son back."

"Damn, cuz, seems like a lot is going on. I am sorry you going through all of that, but you sure it was really like that? He said he was hugging her to calm her down because Noah's mom was coming to kill her and her daughter."

"Well, fuck it, Inaya. I called to ask you to talk to him about letting me have Q so I don't have to take his ass to court, and you on his fucking side."

"Look, Sahnai, your actions lately have been stupid and suspect, but you my family, and I always got your back. I will talk to him and try to get him to see things your way. Just stop fucking up. Why lie and try to be wit' him when you got a whole nigga at home?"

"Because I love him," I simply said before I hung up.

Sitting in bed, holding my teddy bear that Lox bought me way back when we were in Brooklyn and life was simple, I began to cry. Toya wasn't the one who stabbed me, especially since she was the one who saved Kadia. It had to be Honest. I caught him in here staring at me strange, and he was always asking me if I knew who did it and if I saw anything at all that day. Right now he was in DC handling his business, but I had to get rid of that nigga and get away from here. I guessed li'l Q would be better off with his daddy for a while, because I had to get away from Honest's ass. I mean, how did he even know I was hurt or where I was? I never told him I was coming back to Rochester, and I didn't think he knew anyone here.

He always seemed to know where I was. Was he stalking me and that was why he tried to kill me? Was it because he was jealous of Lox and me? I already called my landlord to come and change all the locks, and I was changing my phone number tomorrow morning. If he was the one who tried to kill me, I had to get away. I didn't even feel like I could go to Lox anymore for help. I heard from people how he and Travis's baby's mom, Alani, hooked up. They were just one big happy family with my fucking kid. I never thought he would take another girl besides me seriously.

Seeing a text from Inaya on my phone, I couldn't help but smile.

9:00 p.m. Inaya: Hey, I talked to Lox, and he is willing to give it a chance to see what's up wit' you. He wants to have a little cookout tomorrow with all of us so you can spend the day wit' the kids, and you and him can discuss joint custody.

9:02 p.m. Me: Thanks, cuz, you da best. I promise I won't mess it up this time.

Not waiting for a response, I turned over in my bed, cuddled with my teddy, and went to sleep.

Finally, today I was going to see both Aiden and Q. I missed those boys like crazy and couldn't believe Lox was treating me like a monster or a bad mom. Getting up to shower, I couldn't help but notice the scars on my chest and side from the stabbing. *Damn. I know I have made some bad choices, and maybe I deserve these wounds, this pain. These are the times I wish I had someone to talk to, like a mom, but I ain't got no mother, and I have to accept that. Shit, I never really had a mother.* My mother had drugs and didn't care about me or anyone else. I always had my grandmother, but my grandmother and I were arguing right now because she kept asking me what I was doing with my life, and I hated to say it, but I wondered the same thing. But being stubborn, I just yelled at her and told her to mind her business.

Feeling the water to make sure it was not too hot, I stepped in and scrubbed with my peach-mango body wash from Victoria's Secret. I wanted to make sure I looked better than Lox's new girl, so I made sure my hair was on point. I had it dyed with red and honey blond streaks, and it was long on one side, short on top. My curls and spikes were on point. Stepping into a skater dress by Bebe that was all pink, and throwing on Bebe all-white sandals, I was ready to go. I hoped this shit went well, especially with his mom and sister not talking to me. I was trying to make things better, not worse, so I would apologize to them first and see what happened.

Chapter 39

Inaya

Once again, I was waking up with Kadia in the bed next to me, sleeping, snoring lightly with a little drool on my shoulder. Shit, it brought a smile to my face even though she was wetting up my nightshirt. Since my baby had been back, I couldn't imagine being away from her for even a moment. Unfortunately, Phantom felt the same way, so he was like glue, stuck to our side even though I was still not ready to give him another chance. I couldn't believe I almost lost her because of Phantom thinking so little of me. She was my world, and in the blink of an eye, my daughter could have been gone forever, or I could have been gone forever. Feeling my hand go to my belly, I rubbed my little baby bump, and another smile spread across my face as I thought about a baby with Phantom's black eyes and dimple. I hoped this baby was a boy since we already had a girl, and I was not sure I could survive another "princess" for him to spoil.

Today we were going to Lox's new place. He needed more space for him and the babies, and Azia and the boys basically took over his and Phantom's place since they had been here. Lox was throwing a little barbeque, and he was using it as an opportunity for Sahnai to come see the kids. I thought he wanted us there as a buffer so he didn't strangle her to death. I truly didn't know what was up with her one bit. She was like a different person since she was stabbed, or maybe she had been changed for a long time. This Honest nigga had been around for a while, and I had never even heard of him. It was like he was consuming all of her time. I called and couldn't even talk to my cousin, or she was always "calling me back" and never did. Maybe after today she would realize she missed all of us, especially me and her kids and her niece, and get rid of Honest and come back where she belonged.

Azia and I were very close now. She had been there every day since I escaped from Noah and even took care of me when I'd just gotten out of the hospital with all of my bumps, bruises, and trauma. I had a dislocated shoulder, sprained ankle, bruised vaginal walls, and lacerations on my neck, but I and my unborn baby made it. There were a lot of times I thought we would not make it. Lying on the dirty floor in the abandoned house where Noah was holding me at first made me think he was going to finish torturing me and raping me and leave me there for dead. I was sure that house had some rats that would come and eat me alive. Many days and nights I wanted to give up, and all I could think about was getting my daughter back. Many times when I was ready to give up, I would wish to see Phantom walk through the door, ready to save me. A part of me knew he was coming to save me. I knew he wouldn't stop until he fixed what he did and until he saved Kadia.

"Morning, boo," Azia called out to me as she and all the kids piled into her truck. Once we all made it into the cars, Phantom and I ended up in his Range Rover by ourselves. He had to fight Cordell from coming. He was my little boo, but Phantom be blocking him. I thought he was jealous. I didn't give him any hugs or smiles anymore.

"Yo, ma, you good?" he asked while lightly touching my hand.

"Yeah, I am good, Jah," I responded with a slight smile.

Watching him while he drove, I couldn't help but admire the man he was. Not just his good looks, but his actions. He would die before he let Kadia down, and even though his mistake brought us tragedy, my heart still beat for him. Looking at the shiny spot on his neck that held his newest tattoo, this one of Kadia's name, my mind began to wander. Last night was the first night I stayed home and not with Azia next door. I had not even been over there to clean since Phantom hired a cleaning company so I could rest. Me being the neat freak I was, I was checking on the side of the bed, and I found the letter.

Ever since I read that letter yesterday, I could not stop thinking about Phantom and the words that he wrote. He really touched my soul. He was not the kind of person to tell someone he loved them or he was sorry, but he did.

Iny,

I am writing this letter because you have been gone for over a week now, and I can't take this shit. I still have not found Kadia, and now you are gone. I will not stop until I find you and my baby girl. I refuse to lose another child, and honestly, Iny, I refuse to lose you. I am going to do whatever I have to do. I will tear this city apart if needed to bring you both home. In the process I may not make it home with you, so I want you to understand how much you mean to me. I just want to say it straight out. I love you. I have never loved any girl the way I love you. I love watching you sleep with your hands tucked under your cheek, and the way you smile in your sleep when I kiss you in the morning, and the way you are always singing to me when we are in the car. I know I never told you I loved you, but I tried my best to show it. Once I get you back, I will

*be sure to tell you more, show you more. There
are not enough words to say how sorry I am for
sending Kadia with Noah. I was caught up in being
scared of loving you and my feelings of having my
daughter taken away.*

*Inaya, I want you to understand one thing.
Money is not what makes the world go 'round. It
is people's weaknesses. Some people are weak for
money, drugs, bitches, sex, and for many it's power
and control. Weaknesses turn into addictions and
then become the one thing that consumes them
day and night. For me, I used to be consumed with
money and power and anger, but somewhere along
the way all of that faded into the background, and
you and Kadia became my weakness. I love you.
You make me weak, and I need you.*

   Phantom

I did not think that I could affect him that way, shit,
or at all. He made my emotions crazy. Before I knew it, I
could feel the tears dripping onto my hands. Quickly wip-
ing my tears and hoping Phantom wouldn't see them, I
grabbed his free hand for a moment, mainly to comfort
myself and get my pregnancy emotions in check. I could
tell he wanted to say something but was scared to comment and make me move away with an attitude. I had
been good at pushing him away since he saved me, well,
since he gave my daughter away to that madman.

"Well, looks like Sahnai is already here. I hope she is
behaving herself." I laughed as we got out of the truck. As
soon as we walked in the house, I could feel the tension
in the room between Sahnai and Lox.

"Hey, everyone," I called out as I walked in. Lox came
over and hugged me, and li'l Q walked over to give me a
hug and a sloppy kiss. Sahnai barely acknowledged me.

She just waved in an annoyed way. *Well, fuck her. I don't know what her issue is lately.* She barely even visited me in the hospital. I didn't kiss ass, so she was out of luck. Noticing a short, brown-skinned girl sitting on the couch and chewing on the long end of her honey blond bob, I waited with my hand on my hip for someone to introduce me.

I was really standing that way because this baby had my back hurting. I didn't want her to think I was a bitch, and I didn't want my attitude to affect how our first meeting went, so I offered a smile.

"Dana, this is Phantom's girlfriend, Inaya. Iny this is Dana, Lox's younger sister," Azia introduced us.

"It's nice to meet you," I said with a smile. Instead of a smile, I got piercing green eyes checking me from head to toe and a small laugh.

"I know all about Inaya. I didn't know you were pregnant. I hope you are not telling people this is my cousin's baby," she stated, all the while cutting her eyes at me. Before I could even respond, Lox stepped in trying to defuse the situation, but it was too late for all that shit.

"Dana, what the fuck is your problem? You just met her, and you already have a problem with her? I don't know what is wrong with you since you been back here. You are acting like a bitch. Walking around with your nose frowned up at everybody. You don't even treat your nephews like you interested in them. If you can't behave yourself, you can go home."

"I didn't do anything wrong. I overheard Sahnai talking on the phone about how her baby father supposedly 'raped' her, and she disappeared for weeks and was found with him alive and well. I am sure she was fucking him the whole time. I mean, come on, she is related to Sahnai, and we know the kind of girl she is. I don't want Phantom to fall for no tricks."

"Oh, yeah, Sahnai? You telling people how I got raped? Huh, bitch? My business is community business? What kind of cousin are you? Shit, you supposed to be my best friend and more like my sister. I always had your back. I held you when you cried for your crackhead mother as a kid. I didn't judge you when you hid Q from Lox or when you was fucking Phine for money even after Lox told you to leave him alone, but you quick to stab me in the back?" I screamed at Sahnai as I began crying again. How could my own cousin turn her back on me after all we had been through? Before anyone could make a move, I grabbed the crystal Tiffany vase off the side table and quickly smashed it over Sahnai's head before calmly turning, grabbing Kadia's hand, and calmly walking out the front door.

TO BE CONTINUED . . .